A Conventional Murder

A Rebecca Bauer Hotel Mystery

By Julia Rohatyn

Copyright © 2016 by **Julia Rohatyn**

All rights reserved. No part of this publication may be reproduced, distributed or transmitted in any form or by any means, without prior written permission.

Published by Rachael Goldberg
Neve Ilan
www.juliarohatyn.com

Publisher's Note: This is a work of fiction. Names, characters, places, and incidents are a product of the author's imagination. Locales and public names are sometimes used for atmospheric purposes. Any resemblance to actual people, living or dead, or to businesses, companies, events, institutions, or locales is completely coincidental.

Book Layout © 2014 BookDesignTemplates.com
Cover Design Donna Casey

A Conventional Murder/ Julia Rohatyn‑‑ 1st ed.
ISBN 978-965-92536-0-9
BISAC FIC022040

CHAPTER ONE

Rebecca - Sunday Night

The silvery jet age suitcase that sat beside his massive oak desk meant that he would soon be off on one of his trips to somewhere else where he would be making more money. I guessed that he would be leaving me instructions for special guests in the hotel, but I doubted that any of them would be among the full house that we expected tomorrow for the Bartenders' Association Annual Convention. Maybe he just wanted to warn me to try and leave the hotel in one piece, not such a small request with several hundred bartenders imbibing their own productions.

Visiting his office was always a pleasure, not just because he was such a good man and a good boss, and not just because he had the most amazing view of the curve of the Charles River from the glass wall that covered one side of the office, but because it gave me a chance to delight in all of the works of art. He was a collector, and often changed what was on the walls, for his own pleasure. I was getting to know them, the Renoir and the tiny Rodin statue, and the Wyatt and the Imari jars and bowls and the small blue and gold silk carpet that sometimes hung on the wall and sometimes lay on the wooden floor that had been waxed and buffed. This time it was not to be such a pleasure.

I smiled as he put the file he was reading to the side and looked up at me and shook his head sadly.

"Rebecca, we have a problem, and I wish that this trip were not so urgent, but I can't delay the trip and I can't delay this conversation."

There was no humor in his voice. Clearly, drunken guests were not the issue, and I began to worry.

"You have been accused of taking bribes."

I gulped in amazement and opened my mouth to answer, but at first I was so dumbstruck, I could not think of a word to say. He waited patiently, his blue eyes filled with concern, as he ran his hand repeatedly through his sparse white hair.

"What? What could I possible do that was worth a bribe? Comp a room for a politician? Mr. Hanley, you have known me for years. You know better than that. This is some kind of a sick joke."

"I wish it were." He frowned. "There is someone who claims to have proof that you favored certain produce suppliers for the kitchen in return for, shall we say, favors in return."

"Nothing could be farther from the truth, and I can prove it." I wondered if I could congratulate myself on my habit of saving documents. I kept files for years to help me use history to predict the future, but I wasn't sure that I had all papers that I had found in the kitchen when I began to manage the Treasure Hotel. They were my proof. If I had them.

"Who accused me?"

"You know that I can't tell you that."

"I know that you have to tell me. This is too important to wait until you get back, and I have to know where it's coming from. It's a lie and you know it, so help me find out the why. Please, Jim. I've worked for you for so many years. You know me too well to believe this nonsense. Let's find out and carry on." He sighed and pursed his lips. He began to riffle through the file on his desk, giving me a chance to look at the man who had had been my boss and my mentor, almost since I had started managing hotels. He had remained as fit and thin as he had ever been. Tall and spare, he had developed a very slight stoop. His cheeks were pink, his nose long and thin, and his blue eyes hooded by thick bushy brows that had turned white. He was a perfect image of the Boston aristocrat with a brain that worked like a compassionate computer. I admired him more than anyone else I had ever met. And today he was accusing me of taking bribes. I began to feel sick.

"Against what may be my better judgment, I will tell you. The source of the accusation is Marshall Hammersmith."

I gaped in shock. Marshall was the Reception Manager, one of my department managers in a group of people that I met with every day. I had never done a thing to hurt him. Why was he doing this to me? I'd have to think about this. There must have been something that I had thoughtlessly said or done.

"I am truly amazed. I'm also curious. Marshall has absolutely no connection to the kitchen or to purchasing. If something wrong would be going on there, how could he possibly know?"

"One of the cooks is his cousin."

James Hanley sighed again, his dilemma clear. He had to believe me, but if there was actual proof, I was in trouble.

"I promise to find out what this is all about."

"Now, now, you can't attack this head on. If you have proof, I will have to see it, and I don't want you starting World War Three in my hotel. Subtle, soft, discreet with no frontal attacks, please."

I breathed a tiny breath of relief at the return of his wry humor even if it was minimal.

"I promise." I raised both palms in surrender.

He was right. What he called subtle, I called sneaky. I would have to find out what was going on. I was anxious to leave the elegant, traditional, old master laden office that looked out high over the night lit Charles River, and to rush back to do battle. Unfortunately there was little that I could do. The day was over, but tomorrow I could begin. Conventioneers had already begun to check in, and I hoped that in the organized confusion I would have a chance to get into places that I usually avoided. I had to think and plan and that I could do at home. If Jason had been home, he would have immediately realized that something was wrong, but he was away, and I would not have to fake a good mood.

I rode the elevator down to the street and walked to the subway station totally unaware of my surroundings. Although there was parking in the office tower, I usually chose to leave my Volvo behind, just because of the horrible Boston traffic even on a Sunday evening. At this hour, the 'T' would be empty and I could sit and think while the train rushed through the dark tunnel and clacked rhythmically on the rails.

Marshall had never been my favorite person. I encouraged the managers to spend time together and I could count most of them as friends, or at least as much friends as I could be with people who depended on me for their livelihood. That was the loneliness of the job and that was why I valued having an owner like Jim Hanley. He was a sounding board, a source of advice, a support when things were rough, and now even that was in doubt. But I did have someone else.

I opened my iPhone the minute the train left the tunnel and punched the name that was second on my list.

"Hi, Betsy. I hope it's not too late."

"Uh, uh. What's up?"

"When will you be in tomorrow? I need your help."

"First thing. You had a meet with the big man tonight. Is everything all right?"

"Not really. I need to talk something over with you, to plan a course of attack, but it can wait till tomorrow. Thanks, and sorry for disturbing you."

"Don't be silly. See you tomorrow."

Betsy was the most unlikely looking head of security for the hotel. She was slim and tiny in height, and the long braid that she usually wore hanging down her back made her look like a child, but her 'krav magah' self defense training had made her a real threat to any violent or problematic visitor. She was not only smart, she knew how to lead, and her staff idolized her. I had worked with her in other hotels, and I knew how well she could do her job, but more importantly, she is like family to me and I would be able to count on her, no matter what, or so I thought.

The train stopped just before the turn of Commonwealth Avenue and I realized that if someone else hadn't pushed the stop button, I would have missed it. I stepped down, and looking both ways, crossed the tracks to my street. I walked home barely aware of all the sights of the street that usually gave me so much pleasure. My home, a house that we had inherited from my parents, was also usually a comforting retreat, but after several years of living in the exact same house where I had grown up, Jason had convinced me that we should make it over into a more practical and logical layout. Reluctantly I had agreed, and now my retreat had been replaced by an architectural style magazine showcase. Any appetite that I might have had for a light supper was gone. I made myself a cup of peppermint tea, and sipped. Leaving the half full cup on the table, I headed for bed.

CHAPTER TWO

Rebecca - Monday Morning

I hadn't slept much, but I still felt wide awake and ready for battle, even while realizing that Hanley was right. A frontal attack was not the right way. If it had been anyone else but Marshall, I think I would have just talked with him, to ask if there was some way that I had unintentionally caused pain and hurt, but Marshall was unapproachable. He had no soft edges that I could ever see. I had moved from sick shock to anger and I could have killed him. Instead, I would get Betsy to distract him when the reception office was empty, so that I could snoop in his papers and even in his computer. One time might not be enough, but I was positive that the convention would bring enough problems to keep him busy. My difficulty was that it would keep me busy, too, but I would find a way. The problem was that I didn't really know what I was looking for. I just hoped that there would be some sign.

On an even more practical note, I would also have to make time to search my papers and my computer to find the emails that I sent to the staff when I first came to the hotel. I had received complaints about the low bids that had been ignored. When I had first started to manage the hotel, I had received telephone calls from some of the suppliers. They had told me that although they were positive that their bids had been low, they had never been able to get an order. Hearing that had made me angry and it had made me sad that this was happening. So I asked them to put it in writing, and most of them had done it. Then I waded in and changed the rules, and fortunately, that too should be documented.

As for Marshall, I would prove him a liar, and then I would fire him.

Slipping on a dark gray knee length dress and the matching jacket, I put on makeup quickly, and brushed my mostly untamed auburn curls. Black, gray, or blue suits were more or less a uniform for city hotel managers, but wrinkling my nose at the image in the mirror, I thought spitefully that the males of the profession never had to put on makeup when they were rushing to work. I skipped breakfast, figuring that when I got hungry, I would eat in the coffee shop. I decided to drive to work. It was just past five am and the roads were empty. By the time I could leave the hotel at the end of the day, the roads would be empty again, and if I needed mobility, I preferred to have the car. For inside the city, the car was close to useless, but we stored old files in a storage bin in Watertown, and maybe I would get lucky and have the time to drive there. My search might also lead to suppliers in the suburbs.

It was not that unusual for me to drive to work that early when Jason was away. I would slowly drive down Commonwealth Avenue, watching the pearl-gray morning misted buildings in the distance smudge with color as I approached them. This morning I drove in a tunnel of anger, and determination, and a nauseous feeling in my stomach that I would come to know as gnawing fear. I was sufficiently aware of the traffic lights to stop in time, and of the cars on the road to avoid an accident.

I reached the parking garage, swiped my employee card to open the gate, drove in and stopped short. Jason had begged me to remember to turn off the water before I left for work. He had also begged me to remember to get the garden irrigation computer fixed. I had done neither. The computer could wait, but if I didn't get back home, the sprinklers would sprinkle all day long. I murmured a heartfelt 'Oh, shit' and made a 'U' turn inside the garage and headed back home.

Parking on the street, instead of in our driveway, I got out and went through the narrow opening in the hedge near the stairs that led up to the wide porch which had fortunately escaped the remodeling. The grass was soaking wet. The space where the lilac bush had been uprooted to make way for pretty flowers, and which still felt like a pulled tooth, was a sea of mud. Our neighbor's window was fortunately closed and looked rain-washed. I groaned, turned back to the stairs and ran inside to replace my heels with rubber boots. After I turned off the water, I did what I should have done in the first place. After all, I delegate all the time at work. I sent a message to our gardener, asking her to take care of fixing the timer and adjusting the range of the spray.

Mission accomplished, I calmed down and decided to have cup of coffee and a piece of toast. I wouldn't be able to do anything this early anyway, and my dream of a coffee shop breakfast was just that because later I might be too harried to grab even just a bite. I listened to the morning news and sent an innocuous mail to Jason, signed with x's and o's. It was still early enough to drive with little traffic, and I headed back to Boston.

As I reentered the garage, I saw a taxicab, parked at an angle near the entrance to the lobby. The driver wasn't exactly blocking traffic, but I figured that it would be a good idea to find out what was keeping him from moving. I could also see that the doorman was arguing with the driver, and that was another clue that the situation was urgent. Instead of heading for the garage elevator to the lobby, I hurried back through the parked cars, and ran around the building into the lobby.

Pacing between the reception desk and the revolving door was an elderly female package of total outrage wrapped in an enormous fur stole, unsuitable for our summer weather, and teetering on impossibly high heels. The guest who was trying futilely to leave the hotel was shaped like a furry pouter pigeon. She saw me and exploded.

"Do you actually work here? The doorman is useless. That person in reception promised that my bill would be ready for me. He promised. My cab is waiting. I'll miss my flight and I will sue you all. You do work here?"

There was no one in reception. I stood next to the desk and attempted to calm her down. I knew that we would have her address and her credit card and could send the same invoice by mail or we could have put it under her door if she had asked, and I told her so.

"No, no, no. I want it now and he promised," she sputtered.

"No problem. If you give me your key card, I can use it to bring up the invoice. It will take seconds, and you can be on your way."

As she fished out the card from the depths of an enormous red leather handbag, I continued to speak soothingly. She seemed to deflate and I raced to check the room number and print the invoice. It had been a long time since I worked reception, but it wasn't the first time I had to step in and help and I hoped that I remembered how to do it.

I couldn't get behind the desk. The only way to get in was through the reception office, and when I raced to the passageway and pushed on the door, it was jammed. I pushed as hard as I could. It seemed to give a bit, but not enough to open. Cursing silently to myself, I looked around to see if there was something I could use as a ladder. Obviously, there was nothing, so I dragged an armchair over to the desk, winced and stood on the dark blue and pink upholstery of the heavy mahogany chair and awkwardly climbed over. She looked at me as if I had lost my mind, but shrugged as the computer charged her card and the printer spewed out the bill. Bill, who was the best doorman in Boston, was at her side in seconds and ran with her to the cab. If I had known that the day included gymnastics, I would have worn a pantsuit instead the dress and jacket.

He came back inside. "Whew! What happened to the Hammer? He said he came on shift early, but I haven't seen him since we said hello when I came on myself."

I looked around, puzzled. This wasn't like him at all. I turned to see if he had left any note in the reception office, but the door from reception was locked. What a way to begin the day. The office had two doors, one opening in the hallway, and the one door that opened into the reception but for some inexplicable reason, was locked. The only way for receptionists to get in was through that door, and it was never locked. I climbed out again, and turned to Bill.

"Could you just help me open the other door? It seems to be stuck. If we can't move it, maybe you could climb over the reception desk to get the lock open. It seems to be locked, but that's unreasonable, and I don't want to climb over again.

Bill went through the double doors that led to the passageway and looked through the small round window in the door to the office. With his height he was able to look down at the inside, and he stopped pushing.

"Please call 911. Quick."

"What's wrong, Bill?"

"What's jamming the door is someone on the floor, and there's blood. A lot of blood." He shuddered.

I rushed to the phone and dialed, even now remembering to give our address instead of the hotel name. We had learned the hard way that reporters listen in to police and ambulance scanners and we never wanted that kind of publicity. It had become an automatic habit but we would soon find out that there would be no way to keep the reporters out and some of the guests in.

The first to arrive was an ambulance, and a burly medic who rushed in, only to be met with a door jammed shut. He dealt with the problem with brains and brawn. He grasped the edges of the door and just lifted it off the hinges. Placing the door so that it was leaning against the wall, he bent down to check the supine body. I was still standing next to the desk and I went over and crowded in behind him. He moved the body so that the face was visible.

I leaned on the wall for support. It was Marshall Hammersmith lying on the floor. There was a red-black mark on his forehead and an unhealthy blue white pallor on his face.

Everything seemed to happen at once. A uniformed policeman spun through the revolving door, rushed behind the desk, and grabbed me to shove me out of the way. Then he grabbed the medic. That was more difficult.

Not giving way even an inch, the man turned his head up to greet the onslaught. "I have to check his vitals, man. Get your hands off me,"

"You blind? There's a bullet hole in his head even a dumb cop can see. We gotta wait for the homicide dicks to come. Step away."

I gasped. This can't be happening. Just then, it got worse. A group of four men came through the lobby door. Wearing rumpled suits that looked slept in, they were laughing uproariously, as each one shuffled through papers they held to find their hotel vouchers. Barely glancing at the tableau behind me they thrust the vouchers at me. The shortest, barely topping the counter, smoothed a large blond handlebar mustache, leered at me, and whispered, "Are we the first to get here? We want the best rooms. Four singles on the top floor. We heard they have the best views, although the scenery I plan to look for won't be out the window. We want rooms with double beds." He leered again and smiled.

I smiled back automatically. "You sure are among the first. When did your flight come in?"

"We flew the red eye from LA, ma'am. Happy to be here. Plan to be even happier."

"We have great rooms for you. They're on one of the higher floors. Sorry, the top floor is completely full, but these rooms are really good."

We were holding the top floor rooms for the convention organizers and for solving problems. By problems I mean something far more serious and more demanding than a few early arrivals who had taken too much advantage of the free booze on the flight. If there were no problems to solve, the last guests to arrive would luck out. They would get the last rooms available and these rooms would be on the top floor. The view from up there was really amazing. Fortunately, these guys were too happy and too tired to argue, and after signing in, swiping credit cards, and getting keys they disappeared, and I was back to a frightening reality. I had moved the little machine that coded the keys to the side, and I programmed the room numbers from the other side of the desk, but the computer was almost immovable and someone from the reception department was going to have to do a lot of check-ins during the next few hours.

Standing over the body of my dead Reception Department manager, the medic and the cop were glaring at each other. This was bad and it was about to get worse. In a short while, hundreds of barmen from all over the country would descend on the hotel. If they knew that they were walking into this kind of a mess, they just might turn around and leave. This was a horrible time for any reception manager to kill himself. I hadn't really been able to register what I had seen, but it seemed obvious that it was the missing Marshall Hammersmith and that he had killed himself. I mentally shook myself. In a few minutes, the second receptionist would arrive to help with the convention arrivals and whoever it would be might be in line for a bad surprise. There would be too much work to do alone and he or she would need help. I had to know whom I could call.

"Could one of you gentlemen be so kind and bring me that list tacked on the board over there." The work schedule always included phone numbers, and I had to get a hold of someone from the staff who could help out.

"Sorry, lady. This is a crime scene. No one gets in."

I realized that it was pointless to argue, but I tried. "How can it be a crime scene? It's obviously a suicide. He blocked the door. No one could get in or out."

"Lady, until the inspector says otherwise, it's a crime scene, even if it is a suicide. No one is getting in.

I looked in desperation at the cartons of convention files in the corner. I could get away with waiting until tomorrow to handle distributing the giveaways and fancy bags to the rooms, but I would have to get to them soon, and I still needed the phone numbers. Betsy would also have all of the staff contact information in the hotel security office, and would get them even faster than the airhead who was covering human resources while Patsy, her boss, was on vacation. Worse, perhaps, the receptionist would have to climb in, just as I had, because the only normal way in was through the crime scene. We had to get the office declared as a non-crime scene, and it had to happen fast.

She answered on the first ring. "I'm here. What the hell is going on? The place is swarming with cops."

I groaned. "Come to the lobby and as you run, start calling the reception staff to find someone to help cover."

"I can do that but wouldn't Marshall do it faster. He should be right there."

"Oh, he's here, all right. He's just not doing any talking, ever again."

I heard a splutter on the line and then it went dead. Seconds later she came in on a run and skidded to a stop, looking first at me standing to the side and at the police homicide inspectors who had just walked in through the revolving door.

I felt relieved. The first plainclothes cop, dressed in khaki pants and a sky blue button down shirt that matched his eyes had blond curls cut close to his head in a wheaten gold helmet. He walked in confidently, knowing exactly where to look. Peter was a homicide inspector whom I had gotten to know well when we had a murder in a different hotel, and even better when he and Betsy fell hard for each other and decided to live together. He was thorough and he'd get things done right. Then I felt a frisson of panic. He was thorough, and getting things done right might take a long time.

He was followed by a man who had copied his outfit, but looked entirely different. His gawky body towered over Peter's stocky figure and his angular stride appeared to presage a stumble over his own huge feet. His clothes hung loosely while Peter, even when he had been undercover as a bum, had looked well dressed.

Seeing Betsy near the side of the lobby, Peter swung in her direction, but she caught my glance and waved him away, and he headed towards me. She joined us, and he kissed her on her forehead and me on my cheek. The other man, whom I had never seen before, looked on, bemused, at our social ballet.

"I want to introduce you to Harold Joiner. He has had the misfortune to transfer to our station and I have had the misfortune of getting to show him around." His smile belied the harsh words. "Harold, this is Rebecca Bauer, the primo hotel manager in Boston and this is Betsy Connolly, the chief of security here, and the love of my life." Turning to us, he added, "What is going on? The call we got was mangled. The duty cop didn't realize it was a hotel."

"That was exactly what I wanted. We didn't want any reporters with scanners to hear."

"Hear what?"

My smile disappeared. "Suicide. We have a suicide."

"Your guests would rather die than stay here?"

"Not funny, and it's not a guest. Our Reception manager killed himself inside his office and fell against the door so we couldn't get in. That is, we couldn't get in until the man-mountain medic arrived and removed the door." I pointed in the direction of the office behind the reception desk, where the medic and the uniformed cop were still glaring at each other. "Don't get me wrong. I am upset, but I also really need the two big cartons in the corner of the room. They belong to a convention group that's already started to arrive, and they're asking for their stuff. All the schedules and staff phone numbers are there, too. No one can get behind the desk without climbing over it. If you could just do what you have to do so that we can get back into the office, I would really appreciate it."

"Harold, show us what you can do."

Harold, looking puzzled and nervous, headed for the office where he motioned the cop and the medic away from the door. Peter pulled Betsy away and began to whisper. I stood beside the reception desk, hoping someone would arrive to take over, and pretending that this was a normal procedure.

A stream of people began to walk in through the door and to line up at the desk and I began to check them in. It was a lot easier to say it then to do it. There should have been a stack of files organized by alphabet, but Marshall, who should have prepared them, had been otherwise occupied. For each new guest, I had to fish through the whole pile, find the booking, swipe their credit card, and make a key card for the room that was free. Finding the registration in the computer and checking each guest in would have to wait because the computer was out of reach. The last time I had actually done this alone was years ago, and I was rusty. I was nervous and worried that, without the computer, I would give someone an already occupied room. They were all guests of the convention, and we had calculated how many early checkouts had to be cleaned for them. I whirled around when I saw another hand shuffling the pile of folders, and felt huge relief. Of all the reception staff, Jeri was the best. If Marshall hadn't already been in place when Hanley bought the hotel, I would have picked her to head the department. If Marshall had put her on duty together with him for the morning shift, he had picked the strongest member of the staff and it meant that whoever would have to cope with the majority of the afternoon arrivals would not be the strongest receptionist. That was typical Marshall to make things easy for himself and to hell with the others, but now it was too late to be pissed off at him, again.

"Why are you doing this from the outside of the desk? Where is Marshall?"

I pointed at the armchair. "Climb in, and I'll give you all the bad news."

Jeri looked at me strangely, hitched up her skirt showing long slim legs, took off her shoes, climbed on the chair and maneuvered herself over to the other side. She dropped gracefully to the floor. Before I said a word, she shoved a stack of reservations at me

I alphabetized the files while Jeri handled all the check-ins. Most were men, but there was a smattering of women.

"What should we call them? Barladies, bargirls, barpersons?" I was aware that I was babbling foolishly, and Jeri cut me down.

"Well, boss, I mostly worry that within twenty-four hours we'll be calling them drunken guests."

I sighed because she was probably right. "Remind me why we took this convention."

"We didn't. The guilty party is the reservation department of the chain that used to manage this hotel before Hanley bought it."

"Oh, yeah. It now comes back to me."

"Look, things are under control, now. I'm here, but where is the 'Hammer', and why won't those people let me into the office. We need that stuff for the convention. When the group was booked, the hotel promised to give it out and the organizers will kill us if we don't."

"Ah, yes, that's the bad news." I sighed again. "Speaking of killing, Marshall seems to have killed himself in the office. Those are cops."

She looked at me in horror, and I shook my head sadly.

"You okay, Jeri?"

"I'm stunned. Why would he do a thing like that? I talked to him last night, and he seemed to be in a great mood. I guess you can never tell."

"Right. If you don't need me here, I want to check out what's going on with the cops. They should be finished soon."

I walked around to the side and peeked in. Harold had apparently been talking to the medic, but now he waved him away from the entrance to the small reception office.

He bent down next to Marshall's head and gingerly moved it. Then, fishing out plastic booties from his pocket, he put them on and circled the small room. The wall separating the office from the reception area was mainly taken up by a large electric panel with all the switches for the first floor of the hotel. The main panel was in the maintenance area, but this one covered so many things, it would have been a big problem if we couldn't get to it. There was an empty niche behind the panel and he poked around there for what seemed to be a long time. Then he called out for Pete, who walked quickly into the room after putting on booties. They both circled the room. With two large men inside, along with the two desks, Marshall's and another for any receptionist who needed an additional place to work away from the desk in the lobby, and two high backed wheeled desk chairs, there was a tight fit, but they circled around each other, opening drawers and cabinets, sweeping their gloved hands over shelves.

Meanwhile, Betsy and I stood together as close as we could get to watch was going on. Finally, Pete walked out of the room and stood facing us.

"Harold, we need the crime scene people here right away. Call them, okay. Ladies, sorry, but we can't let you in the office."

"Honey, this is getting to be ridiculous. When can we have the office back?"

"Hopefully, tomorrow."

"What!" We both shouted in unison.

"Keep it quiet, for now, but this is no suicide."

"What? How?" I sputtered.

"Well, first of all, there is almost no powder burns. It's pretty hard to shoot yourself if you hold the gun far away. It's possible, but I've never seen it. He's been shot right in the middle of his forehead. That's difficult to do to yourself, and there's worse."

"You said a gun? Where would he get a gun? I had no idea. Maybe he did hold it away from himself. He blocked the door. How could anyone get in or out? What could be worse?"

"Slow down. He was shot, and there is no gun here. That's the worst. You don't believe that he shot himself and then got rid of the gun? Someone else did it. Fact."

I sighed, trying to absorb all this and to figure out what it meant, but I couldn't get focused. "How could someone get in and out?"

"That part's easy. Did you know that there's a ladder here behind the electric panel?"

"Sure, but it doesn't go anywhere. They just store it there."

Betsy, who had been silent until then, piped up. "There's a trap door. It leads to a closet in the mezzanine floor above us where the administration offices are. Hardly anyone knows about it, but we know. We check it every now and then."

Until this second I had nursed a bubble of hope that we could soon put this mess behind us. The trouble was that it was not a mess. It was a real live person who had been murdered. It was a pretty, foolish, and callous bubble, and it had just burst, filling me with dread. This was so not good for me. Of course, it was worse for Marshall, but he was past caring. The cops would be looking for people who had a reason to want Marshall dead, and that would be me. There was no way that Hanley would keep quiet. It was only a short way from that to a realization that at best my career was shot and at worse I could be accused of an actual crime. That would have been reason enough, in some people's minds, to get rid of Marshall.

I had disliked him almost from the beginning. When we took over the hotel, Hanley had told me not to fire anyone until I had given them a chance. I had given him a chance. Most of the staff from the other department seemed to like him, his own department somewhat less. They called him "the Hammer" and he took it as a compliment, but I thought he was lazy. He would arrange the work schedule to give himself the easiest shifts. He handled guests with ease, but didn't seem to like them as people, and the perceptive ones noticed. He wasn't bad enough to fire or good enough to like. Now he was dead and I had no idea who, aside from myself, could have wanted to do away with him, and I hadn't really wanted him dead, just gone.

Still, I had a window of time, until Hanley got back. I was pretty sure that he had kept the accusations to himself, but when he found out about the murder, he would tell the story and I was done for. I would have to prove that Marshall was lying. It would be even better if I could find out why. Then I would have had no reason to kill him.

"Earth to Rebecca, come in."

I jumped. "Sorry, I was..."

"Yeah, I know. It's that feeling that we should be looking over our shoulder."

The realization flooded in. Whoever killed Marshall knew about the ladder and the trap door above, and so it was probably someone who worked in the hotel. Could we also be in danger?

"Are you worried, Betsy?"

"It could just as well be someone who used to work here before we came, but yes I am concerned, okay, worried. This is really going to mess us up. Everyone's gonna suspect everyone else, and they're gonna start turning on each other."

"And there is that unpleasant fact that someone is killing managers."

"Come on. One manager and..."

In that second, my telephone clicked an announcement of a new message, and Betsy's phone beeped.

CHAPTER THREE

Betsy - Monday Morning

This started out as a glorious joyous day. Living together had meant combining our meager furnishings, but we had just begun to buy things together. The new mattress had arrived, but without the bed, so we had slept on the floor. We woke up early enough to turn over and go back to sleep, but instead we began to talk. We exchanged gossip about the next door neighbor, exclaimed over his trips to Japan and Thailand, and began to talk about arranging schedules for our next vacation. Then, we began to talk about how it should really be a honeymoon because we both wanted to spend the rest of our lives together. And there we were.

With an abashed smile, Peter got out of bed and brought me a cup of coffee. Coffee in bed was something I liked and he hated, so it was especially appreciated. I drank the coffee slowly while he watched. When the cup clinked, I sipped more carefully, trying to hide the wide grin that spread over my face, until I caught the glint of the diamond ring he had dropped into the coffee. When I fished it out and licked it clean, we both began to laugh.

"I hope that it fits right. I stole your birthstone ring to get the measure."

I began to cry, and his eyes opened wide in panic.

"No, it's okay," I gasped, putting it on my finger. "It's just joy. A surfeit of joy."

We held each other, alternating kisses with giggles, until it became so late that we had no choice. We had to wash and dress and run to work. I found an old gold chain in my jewelry box and threaded the ring on it. It would stay around my neck for the next few days, till we were ready to make an announcement to our families. My mom and his parents would be the first to know, but until we made definite plans I couldn't tell my mother. She would have the church booked and the invitations printed by nightfall. I knew how happy she would be. She loved Peter. Sometimes it seemed that she thought he was too good for me. So, wow!

Breakfast at the hotel staff dining room meant that I could skip eating, but Peter grabbed a day old bagel with cream cheese and munched as we walked out the door.

Peter dropped me off at the hotel, and before I could even float to my office, Rebecca called. She asked a strange question about work schedules in reception and offered an even stranger comment about Marshall not talking. Every time Rebecca has a problem that she can't solve, she calls me. It's usually flattering to know how indispensable I am, but today I had really wanted to be alone with myself to prolong the euphoria before my immersion in the day-to-day turmoil.

I turned around and headed for the lobby. I wouldn't say anything. I didn't think I could trust her to resist the temptation to tell and then Mom would find out. There was a time when I could tell her anything, and usually did, but that kind of trust should be mutual. Since she had started to manage this hotel, it wasn't. It had bothered me, but I had completely put it behind me because I had no choice. Something was wrong between us, but we still had to work together.

I foolishly figured that I could deal with whatever problem she had, return to my office, and go back to enjoying the day.

As I reached the lobby, I saw that something was missing. One of the arrangements of four armchairs placed around a coffee table was missing a chair and it stood next to the reception desk. I headed over to pull the heavy chair back in place and then saw Peter coming through the wide revolving door, wearing a puzzled look, and accompanied by Harold, the newbie who had transferred from Waterways and Docks. Peter, who had been saddled with introducing him to the area, had told me that he was a nice guy but that he didn't have a clue about homicide or major crimes.

We headed towards each other, like two opposite magnetic poles, and then, glimpsing Rebecca near reception, I swung away towards her. Peter, seeing my shift, headed for her also. We all ended up near the reception desk and exchanged friendly pecks on the cheek, all around. Peter introduced us to Harold, and asked about the call from the hotel. That's when the day went to hell.

CHAPTER FOUR

Rebecca - Monday Morning

"Fire in Main Ballroom, section B, " announced the automatic fire control. I realized that a notice had also gone out to all of the department heads, and to the fire department. Betsy was faster. She snaked an arm into the off limits reception office and snagged the fire extinguisher.

"Hey!" The two detectives and the uniformed policeman shouted, but she was gone. I ran after her, detouring into the small alcove used by the bellboys, to grab another red fire extinguisher. As we burst into the center of the ballroom, separated by huge sliding wall sections from the right third that was set up as a dining room, and the left that was a meeting room, we faced a scene of hallucination. The barmen's convention had set up a trade fair, presenting every imaginable uniform, glassware, cocktail shaker, novel sorts of liqueur and liquor, and gadgets that a barman could want. Each booth was the expression of its owner's creativity, from science fiction and aliens to a Hawaiian luau and an Italian vineyard. Facing us on the opposite wall was a medieval kitchen with a huge fake fireplace that was quickly going up in flames. The plastic material had turned to flaky soot that floated in the air. Tiny black snowflakes began slowly and gently to settle on a pile of rainbow colored bar aprons, on an artistically arranged pile of tiny beer kegs, on a huge wine barrel, on stacks of white dishes awaiting their load of croissants and Danish pastries, on the gold and cream chandeliers and on the blue and gold pile of the carpet. A group of three sales reps huddled nearby. They were transfixed in horror, neither fleeing nor shouting an alarm.

Betsy, Potter, the chief engineer who had joined the fray, and I all attacked the flames with foam. I looked at the ceiling nervously. The instant the heat reached the right temperature, the sprinklers would go into action, and the room would turn into a soaking mess, damaged more by water than by fire.

Little by little, the flames got smaller and smaller and finally drowned in foam.

"I'll cancel the fire department," Potter muttered in his thick Russian accent as he left the room. We were left to face the trio of frightened sales reps. One was a woman wearing elegant gold tipped stiletto heels, a bright red skirt that defied the law of physics that said that two objects could not occupy the same space in the same time, and a pink low cut blouse. She was surrounded on each side by two balding men, dressed in a male parody of her costume with pink shirts and bright red jackets. They paled in comparison to her, and they spent most of the time alternating between staring at the spectacle of the burning fireplace and trying to peek down their colleague's décolletage.

I faced them sternly, but before I could open my mouth, Betsy burst out, "What were you thinking? You planned to wait till the whole place went up in smoke? What the hell did you do?"

"We just wanted to get rid of the wrappings from our lunch," one of the two almost identical men stammered. "We though it was a real fireplace. It looked like a real fireplace, so I threw a match in. It should have been a real fireplace."

Betsy ground her teeth.

"It is quite obviously not a real fireplace," I answered in as calm a voice as I could muster. "As you can see, there is quite a mess, and I would like all three of you to notify your companies that I intend to charge them for the cleanup and the damage. I couldn't care less if they pay themselves, or charge you."

The woman puffed herself up to protest, but thought better of it and shut up. Betsy and I took their cards and left.

Outside the ballroom, we stopped and looked at each other.

"Boss, I don't know whether to laugh or cry."

"I don't know about that, but I am personally still shaking."

"I can't believe it's not even ten o'clock. What a day this is turning out to be, and it hasn't even started."

"You have no idea. Hundreds of barmen and women are arriving and we have to set up a welcome cocktail for this afternoon, with entertainment, no less, and it was supposed to be in there. We'll move it next door and they can squawk as much as they want. Thank god, they have a tour of Boston and a dinner on the docks. The real fun starts tomorrow when we have to have the room ready."

"That's good. I was afraid you planned to try and get out of dinner tonight."

CHAPTER FIVE

Rebecca - Monday Afternoon

Having dinner with Betsy, Pete, and Bridget, Betsy's mom, along with the youngest three of her brothers, was the absolutely last thing I wanted to do, but I could see no way that I could get out of it without arousing suspicion or without arousing the potentially formidable ire of Betsy's mother. What I really wanted to do was get through the day somehow and spend the evening looking for old memos and emails, but it would have to wait. If I could find proof that instead of taking bribes, I had prevented them, I would feel enormous relief, but now that was sadly postponed. Before the family dinner, I would have to get through the rest of the day.

There are several ways to handle paperwork. Sometimes it's pure garbage that gets trashed without a second thought. Sometimes there is the stuff that requires no answer and will never be needed again and can get thrown away after some thought. There are letters and files that are neither urgent nor critical and that can be safely put into a pile for the next day. When the next day comes, you actually have to deal with them. Sometimes, if you leave something in that pile long enough, it turns into the second category and you can throw it away with only a tiny qualm of regret or guilt. Mostly, however, paperwork is something that you don't have to love, but you do have to do. Most of the rest of the day was spent answering urgent mail, and some of that was mail that someone else considered urgent.

The reservation department handled all kinds of reservations all on their own. There were individuals and groups and conventions that were standard, but there were also bookings that lit red lights and these would come to me for approval. For one example, I never would have taken the barmen. Not that I have any objection to them personally, or to bars in principle, but I would have realized that we would have to keep regular guests away. If we had our normal kind of visitor together with a bunch of carousing, often drunk young men and women, the others would never come back again. If we couldn't fill the hotel with the convention, we would have to break a taboo and leave empty rooms. This time, I hoped we would come out more or less okay, failing more bonfires, but there never was going to be a next time. That was the kind of decision I had to make all the time and that I found on my desk, the kind of decision that couldn't be put off.

Then there was my playing King Solomon for two arguing staff members. That happened often enough and this was one of these days. At some point, Milly walked in. She stood opposite me with her hands on her slim hips and raised her eyebrows. Milly, who is almost old enough to be my mother and who I think is one of the best possible secretaries in the world, ordered me a sandwich, after tut-tut-ting over my forgetting to go to the dining room for lunch. I almost never see her eat, and her figure shows it. Always dressed in a knee-length straight skirt in some shade of gray and a sweater twin set in varying shades of blue, with her white blond hair swept back in a French chignon, her elegantly curved light brown eyebrows and icy blue eyes, she could fit well in a fashion magazine of the fifties.

Finally, I was able to go to the cocktail party for the bar people. On the small stage that we had set up, a singer in a slinky long silver gown was crooning something slow and melodic, accompanied by a bass player and a pianist with a keyboard. There was barely enough room for them, and I hoped that she wouldn't be singing anything more energetic. I was barely through the door, when I saw one of the convention organizers barreling my way with fire in his eyes. The fat little bald man with a toothbrush mustache was trembling with anger, and I was pretty sure that I knew why. I had found him irritating and unpleasant in every part of the negotiations, but this time he had a reasonably good excuse not to be happy.

Breathless from the exertion he gasped, "I cannot tell you how perturbed I am. Perturbed. I walked in and was amazed to find that you people have not lived up to your commitments. Amazed, I went up to my room to check all the correspondence just to be positive, and it is positive that I am. I do not want to complain, but."

I interrupted him. "But you will." I smiled happily.

In my irritation with him, I found that I could not remember his name. I simply blocked it out. It was something like Bramskso, or Brimsko, so I mumbled something ending with 'sko'.

"Mr. Umphsko, I am fully aware that this cocktail party was to have taken place next door with the trade show, so that the exhibitors could show their wares. You will notice that there are tables lining the wall, and that there are displays there, and I know that this minimalist approach was not what you had in mind, but, believe me that we did have the best interest of your guests at heart. Please come with me and I will show you what your exhibitors have done to our meeting hall."

With a puzzled expression on his face, he followed me to the door that led to the disaster scene next door. I opened the door, but prevented him from walking in.

"I don't want you to get soot on your clothes," I explained.

He looked in and opened his mouth in surprise. Potter was kneeling near the fake fireplace, fixing an electric outlet. Three men in Housekeeping Department uniforms were cleaning. One was vacuuming the carpet, one was scrubbing part of the wall, and one walked from table to table with rags and a bowl of cleaning solution.

"I hope that you will appreciate that we will not charge you for the damage, since we were able to catch the perpetrators in the act, three of your exhibitors. They will have to pay."

He flustered and stammered and fled back into the cocktail party without even a word of apology. For the short time that I was at the party, he avoided me by skittering away whenever I was close by.

I saw his partner, who had not even realized that something was amiss. He greeted me with a broad smile and requested that I participate in the photogenic toast to a successful convention for the photoshoot that the convention organizers had organized.

By that time, the convention goers themselves couldn't have cared less. We had given them the beautiful hors d'oevres and expensive alcohol that they had ordered and paid for but they seemed oblivious to those as well. Samples of the trade show lined a wall, but almost none of them paid any attention. They must have started drinking in their rooms, because most of them seemed inebriated. I wandered among them, smiling and laughing, broke free, got in my car and headed for Bridget's house, late, but forgivably late.

The Connolly dining room was so familiar to me that I didn't even have to look around to notice that she had taken out the good china from the glass-fronted cherrywood hutch that took up most of the wall to the right. Facing the entry was a large bay window that looked out over the apple tree and the lilac bushes in the back yard. The table, part of the same set that I remembered from so many dinners during my childhood, could seat the ten members of the family easily with space left over. Bridget had been my mother's caretaker for the long hard years before Mom left us for good, and that care-taking extended to melding a bookish lonely Jewish teenager into the rambunctious slew of Irish Connolly kids.

This evening, only two kids were missing. Mary was already married with her own crew to feed, and Liam had been given a pass to go a birthday party from his class. Bridget was still an amazing cook, and you can take it from me, because I have a history of dealing with some of the top Boston chefs. The tomato and cabbage soup was probably ambrosial, but it was wasted on me. While the twins told funny stories about school, I mechanically laughed when everyone else laughed, but in my mind I was somewhere else. I was counting the many places that I would have filed letters of complaint from food suppliers who felt that they could give the best price and still never get the order. This was enough years ago, that the letters would not be easily accessible. Then I planned a method for retrieving the old emails that I had sent to my chef telling him that I wanted periodic price quotes for the supplies that we bought almost every day, and that for equal quality we were going to start taking the best quote. I was pretty sure that I had not erased any of them. Hanley had just bought the hotel, I was new, and I was sure that that the chef was not going to like being told what to do, not by anyone, not by a newcomer, and certainly not by a woman.

The next course was served by Bridget, with help from Betsy. There were huge platters of thin slices of pot roast, simple enough on a menu but food for the gods when Bridget cooked, and heaps of mashed potatoes and candied yams and butter drenched broccoli. I knew from experience how good it all tasted, but it might as well have been straw. I vaguely realized that the reason for the feast was Pat's visit home from college in California, and he told us all about it. Bridget had hoped that he would choose Boston College, because she wanted him close by. When he had told her that he wanted to go to Loyola Marymount, we had all feared an explosion from Bridget. We all knew that she dearly wanted him to study in a nearby university, and she usually did not keep her desires bottled up. To our surprise, her suspicions had been fixed on something else entirely, and our fears were located in the wrong place. He had decided on a school with a famous theological department, and his deepening interest in the priesthood had her chewing her nails.

"If a son of mine chose the church twenty years ago, I would have been over the moon," she had said to me. "It's different now. There aren't enough priests, so they move them around, and there isn't enough money so everything is harder. I'm keeping my fingers crossed, but in the end he'll do whatever he wants to do." She had shaken her head pensively.

This day, the mood was festive and humorous. Everyone knew why they were laughing except for me. I had moved over to the 'what if' stage. What if I couldn't find the emails? They were from years ago and there had been several upgrades in my computer. Sometimes when our computer people do an upgrade, stuff is lost. They claim it isn't so, but I know that they are wrong. Once there was a settlement in the battle over how purchasing for the kitchen was going to be handled, there would have been no reason to save the letters. What if I had thrown them out, deleting them from my computer? It was entirely logical to get rid of them. I could prove that the meal costs had gone down, from what they had been before I came, but even I knew that there were so many ways to explain that. What if they all realized that food cost was not proof of anything. I chewed mechanically, and somehow realized that I was wasting very good food.

Even I, in my dissociated state, couldn't ignore the double barreled dessert of chocolate cake and a fruit salad that reeked of Grand Marnier. The combination was so heavenly that no one spoke. Everyone was busy eating. This had been a simple, homey, delicious meal, and almost every bit of it had been wasted on me.

Amid fervid declarations of thanks, everyone rose, and prepared to depart.

"Rebecca, stay just a minute."

I had the feeling that I was busted, so everyone left and I remained to face the music.

CHAPTER SIX

Betsy - Monday Evening

I've been walking on eggs since Rebecca began to manage here, and I hoped that the family dinner would change things back to where they used to be. No such luck. Rebecca's body came to dinner, but the rest of her was somewhere else. As usual, Mom had prepared a feast, maybe even more than just a feast, because Pat had come home for a visit. Little did she know about the other reason to celebrate, but that would come soon enough. I still hadn't said a word about our engagement, and the ring was safely hidden under my bulky sweater. As usual, the food was marvelous, but Rebecca was just going through the motions. I don't think that she was even aware of what she was eating. I realized sadly that nothing could come back to being like it was.

When Mom had gone to work taking care of Rebecca's mother before she died, we had more or less lived in each others' houses. The connection remained. Rebecca was my sometime babysitter at first and then she was my big sister. She remained my big sister when she convinced me to come back to Boston and to run security in her hotel. She had been my big sister when she introduced me to Mr. Hanley and he gave me a job checking out his planned purchase. She remained my big sister until Mr. Hanley finally decided to buy the hotel and to make her the manager of the newest hotel in a chain that did not allow staff from the same family to work in the same hotel.

I expected to be fired but I hoped that I would be transferred to another one of the hotels. I waited and waited and nothing happened, except that somehow in subtle ways Rebecca stopped being my big sister. I didn't know if she had lied. No, I couldn't imagine her lying but I could see her shading the truth to her boss about our relationship. I tried to convince myself that the rule only counted for biological sisters, although that seemed silly to me because it would contradict the reason for the rule. I was only sure that she had not asked for special treatment because that was something that she never ever did.

So I remained in my job, bummed out because I really loved Rebecca but she didn't seem to care about me in any way except as an employee.

The atmosphere at the dinner was warm and celebratory for my family, but totally weird between me and Rebecca, so I was relieved when Mom signaled me to get lost after we had barely finished our coffee. I grabbed Peter's arm and pulled gently.

"What's up?"

"We don't have to stick around. Let's drive home, park the car, and go for a walk around the Fenway. We could use some exercise to work off this dinner."

"What's really wrong?" Peter knows me too well to fall for my cheery demeanor.

"Mom just signaled me. I think, I hope, she wants to talk to Rebecca. If anyone can figure out what is going on with her, it's Mom. So let's make tracks fast."

We put on our coats and left, while the rest of the family scattered, some to their rooms upstairs, and some to meet friends, leaving Mom alone with Rebecca

.

CHAPTER SEVEN

Rebecca - Monday Night

"The tea kettle is on. Do you want a cup?"

"Sure. Thanks."

She put two cups and saucers on the table and poured the fragrant steaming tea.

"Sugar? Lemon? Milk?"

"Just lemon, thanks."

She put two slices of lemon on a small plate for me and poured a smidgen of milk in her cup. My tea was too hot to drink. I should have taken the milk.

"What on earth is the matter?" Bridget looked at me severely.

"The tea is a bit too hot."

She looked at me as only Bridget can, and shook her head.

"Rebecca..." She said sternly.

My answers came from in dribbles and then in a gush.

"I had a pretty bad meeting with my boss."

"You have a boss? I thought you were the boss."

"You know what I mean. The owner."

She waited.

"Someone accused me of taking bribes."

"Oh, my word. Did you take bribes?"

I answered with indignation. "Of course not."

"So?"

"He didn't dismiss it."

"Did he tell you who accused you?"

"He didn't want to."

More silence.

"I got it out of him and it was one of my department managers, and Hanley is away for a while, but he committed suicide, the one who accused me, not Hanley, except Peter said it was murder, not suicide, and when Hanley comes back, they'll know that it was me. I don't mean me who killed him, but me who had a reason to kill him."

"Stop! Calm down and tell me about it. From how you looked I thought you maybe had a fight with Jason."

"Jason's away, thank God. He would have really killed Marshall."

"You mean Marshall, that smarmy person in reception?"

"That's the one." I paused, trying to get all the scattered pieces of me back together.

"Bridget, I am really scared. You don't have to be guilty to get arrested, or tried, or even convicted. Even if I can prove that I didn't take bribes, I still have a super good reason to be mad at Marshall. I don't know what to do."

"Can I make a suggestion? You know the best thing about advice is that you don't have to take it, but do listen."

I nodded.

"First of all, you need a good criminal lawyer. I'll check that out for you. I think that I have the perfect solution. Then, find your old emails and letters, and then find the real murderer."

I gaped at her. "The police have to do that. What can I do to catch a murderer?"

"There is no one who knows how that hotel works better than you. Use that to figure out who it could have been, assuming that it has anything to do with the hotel. It might not. It could be entirely personal, in which case there is little you can do."

My face sagged.

"Cheer up. Chances are that there is some connection and you can find it if anyone can."

"I don't know as much as I thought I did. The killer escaped through a trap door that I knew nothing about. Betsy knew. Sometimes the manager is the last person to know. Everyone hides things from the boss. That trap door leads to a closet near my office, and I didn't know."

"You know more than you think you do, and Betsy will help you."

"She can't work against Peter."

"If she doesn't believe you, she won't help you, and if she does, she will. It has nothing to do with Peter. That's just how she is."

"Um," I muttered doubtfully. "All right, but please let me be the one to tell her what's going on. I'll try to find a way that won't put her in an impossible dilemma."

"What kind of dilemma would that be?"

"If she tells Peter before it's the right time, I could be in serious trouble, and if he asks her if she knew, there is no right answer for her. She won't lie, but he will be furious if she did know and kept it secret. I don't know, Bridget. The more I think about it the worse it gets."

"Rebecca, get it together," Bridget said strictly. "You can figure out who could have known about the trapdoor."

"Anyone who had been told. But you're right. Anyone could have known, but saying that is pointless. There are people who definitely would have known. That would be anyone who works or used to work in reception, and anyone who works or used to work in security. I would eliminate security. I can check with Betsy, but I bet she was the one who ordered them to regularly check the trap door, and also we check them out pretty carefully before we hire."

"Slow down. Anyone with a good enough motive can kill, so don't be so quick to eliminate. But see; now you're cookin'."

She smiled at me and I, rather tentatively, smiled back.

"You know a lot about computers, much more that Betsy. Can you find out what he was doing from his?"

"Quite a lot, I imagine, but I bet the police have taken it. The office is off limits to us."

"Well, can't you tell them that you need the computer because of business things, reservations and stuff like that?"

"Not if they know anything about it. We have everything on the main system. It would have to be. The Reservation Department takes the booking, and the receptionist checks the people in, and housekeeping cleans the rooms, and F and B cooks and serves their food."

I hit my forehead in sudden realization. "Wow, am I am being stupid. I can get at anything he was doing, except for emails and internet. I can get at anything he saved because we back up on the main server. Bridget, you are a genius."

"Saying is not the same as doing, but it is a start. There is something else, isn't there?

I shook my head. Weren't murder and blackmail enough?

"Is there something going on between you and Betsy?"

"I have no idea what you mean. Has she said something?"

"My daughter doesn't have to tell me for me to see what's bothering her. You're her boss. That can't be comfortable."

"This isn't the first time we've worked together. I was her boss at the Mall Hotel before."

"Yes, Becca, but now you both work together a hotel that doesn't allow family members to work together."

I sighed in relief. Bridget was imagining a problem that didn't really exist. When Hanley asked me to manage his newest hotel, we had a lot of strategy meetings and the issue of Betsy came up. I was honest with him, and anyway he already knew. I wanted Betsy for the Security Department because she was so good, aside from the fact that she was already in place, but she was just like a sister. I knew about Hanley's rule, and I thought it was the right policy, so I prepared myself for dealing with a replacement. Hanley saw it otherwise. I remember exactly what he said. 'You are smart enough to handle it. Don't be too easy on her and don't be too hard on her. She stays.'

I was relieved, but I wasn't sure it could work. I shouldn't have worried. I tried to treat Betsy like any of the other managers and most of the time it worked really well. Bridget was a worried mother. I would have to find the right way to explain it to her. I was positive that Betsy understood.

"Hanley knows about us, and actually he convinced me that it should work. I really try very hard to stay right on the fence. Not to favor her and not to be too hard on her. Actually it's pretty difficult to be tough with her. Betsy is just great at her job."

She shook her head sadly. "That's nice to hear. But, you know, God created speech for us. He intended for us to use it."

"Evolved." I said in the automatic reflex response of a sally in an ancient war that I could never win. I could never win because I based myself on doubt and Bridget based herself on certainty.

"Whatever, Rebecca," she said. "Speech was created or evolved so that we could communicate with each other. Thinking something, thinking it very hard and intensely, doesn't make it known to anyone else. Obviously, I'm not talking about 'hello', 'goodbye', 'see you tomorrow'. Perhaps you're trying a little bit too hard and she feels it as a strain between you without understanding why. She doesn't understand because there's been no communication between you. Try to communicate. Try to make real contact with her, and ease up on yourself. It might be better all around, and you should know that she really loves you.

"I do know but I also think you're wrong about her misunderstanding. I'll give communication a try."

"You're not going to like the next piece of advice. Go home. Try to get a good night's sleep. You'll be much sharper in the morning. The world won't end if you don't start right this instant."

"It actually might end for me, but you are probably right."

So I went home, sure that I would not be able to sleep. From door to bed took only minutes. A goodnight call to Jason, where he was in midmorning, toothbrush, cholesterol pill, and out like a light. Strange dreams of computer programs and long weird letters, and jails with bars on the windows, but sleep for all that.

CHAPTER EIGHT

Rebecca - Tuesday Morning

I woke up at five with a start, fully awake, not one bit sleep deprived, and ready for battle. Maybe in the movies, when you get all psyched up for war, you get to actually fight someone, but in real life, the timing can be off. I walked through the employee entrance before the morning shift had started, and I was sure that I would be alone at that early hour. Apparently everyone had set their alarm-clocks early, and I had to wade through all the people who amazingly appeared from nowhere, and seeing me, wanted something from me.

Jenny, from security, checking in the staff arriving for the morning shift, had a bright smile to welcome me, and a complaint about the number of night shifts she got.

"You'll have to take that up with Betsy. You know that she does the schedule. If you feel that she's been unloading too many nights on you, talk to her first to see if you can work it out."

"Oh, no. It comes out very even, and that's the problem. I need the extra study time. I want more nights."

I made a face at her. "Betsy. Okay"

"Yes, Ma'am. Have a great day." She smiled and it was fortunately clear that she took no offense.

As I walked away, I looked back at her. Darker and taller than Betsy, she still had copied the long braid hanging down her back and the pink lipstick. She could do worse than take her boss as a role model.

I passed by the storeroom and peeked in. If I ignored John, who had worked there since the hotel was opened, he would be insulted, but if I stopped to say hello, the conversation would be awash with a torrent of complaints and it would take an hour that I didn't have. I sometimes thought that these many injuries that he suffered were actually his main joy in the job. I breathed a sigh of relief when he was not visible through the small glass window.

I headed for the elevators and instead of riding up to the lobby or to my office, I decided that before I could do the serious work that lay ahead, I should check what was happening in the guest floors. As the elevator doors opened on the third floor, I saw a tall, skinny, blond young man of about twenty-three or -four years old, covered in freckles, in white boxer underwear, and nothing else. He was jamming his key card into the lock repeatedly, and cursing colorfully.

"Excuse me, Sir. Can I help you?"

He was so busy cursing and yelling that he didn't hear me. I tapped him on the shoulder and he jumped, facing me. Unshaven and bleary-eyed, he had trouble focusing.

"I got locked out and the damn key won't work."

"Let me try to help, Sir. Just wait a minute and I will get you into your room. What is your name?"

"William Riley, ma'am. I would apprecy, appeasey, aw fuck. If you can help me, please do."

Pretending to ignore the fact that our guest was both pickled and almost naked, I called Reception and asked for the room number, which turned out to be, of course, the room opposite. I took the key card from him, gently turned him around to face the correct room, opened the door, and watched him walk in and flop face-down on the bed. I placed the key card on the desk, closed the door, and walked away.

The rest of the tour was fairly uneventful. Outside one of the housekeeping pantries on the floor that I was checking, there was a group of maids who were getting their carts ready to clean rooms. They included a Russian, two Puerto Ricans and a girl from China, and the humor united them. As they loaded their carts with sheets and pillowcases, and checked that they had enough cleaning materials, they were giggling together over the state of undress of some of the barmen wandering the corridors. I raised an eyebrow, but in truth I thought it was pretty funny, too. There had to be something funny about the disastrous convention that we were hosting.

As I turned towards my office, I bumped into Betsy.

"My Mom said you wanted to talk with me."

I mentally cursed at Bridget. She was incapable of letting things happen by themselves. "Yeah, but it can wait. I'll see you later."

She turned away, wearing a puzzled expression, and I cursed again. Once in the office, I barely sat down before Milly brought me a mug of coffee.

"I'd like to try to get in a few hours of quiet work. Emergencies, only, okay?"

"Absolutely. I'll do the best I can."

Blessedly, I knew that her best was very good, and that she could handle almost anything thrown at her. The computer was on, waiting, and I decided to try the emails first. I opened up all the sent mails from as far back as I could. I almost never erased sent mail, and after only a few minutes of searching I found a group of emails sent long ago to the chef, informing him that I would require a comparison of price quotes for any purchases over a thousand dollars, and regular scheduled comparisons of price quotes for the whole market list. When I had written the mails, I had no problem visualizing his reaction. For someone unused to this way of working, it would be a real pain in the neck. I had really thought it was the right way to go, and it was the way all the purchasing was done in every hotel where I had worked before, but the catalyst had been the group of letters and phone calls from a number of suppliers who had heard that there was new management in the hotel. They all told the same story. No matter how low their quote, they never got the order. If it had been only one, I might have thought that low quality was the reason, but six? Pure sign of funny business going on, and I had a problem. Hanley had heard stories about the hotel staff, and so had I, but he had asked me to give everyone of them a chance. 'Everyone' included the chef who would have been difficult to replace in any case. I never dreamed that it was the whole kitchen staff, but it was beginning to look like that was the case. One of them, apparently, was Marshall's cousin, and he, alone or with others, had reason to be angry enough to want to get revenge.

Anyway, now that I had the first step, I could prove that I had acted to prevent kickbacks, but it wasn't nearly enough. I needed the original letters to prove that there actually had been kickbacks before I began to manage the hotel. The first place to look was in received mail. It should have been filed or erased long ago, but I had the not uncommon bad habit of leaving incoming mail, just in case, and even though it was years ago, it just might still be there. It wasn't.

Then I searched in email files and then in document files. I read every single page from the purchasing files and the food and beverage files. In desperation I began reading miscellaneous files. I had put a lot of jokes there, good ones that even now made me laugh, but I was closer to tears than to hilarity.

I went back to received mail again, thinking that perhaps it wasn't as long ago as I thought. Maybe I had received the letters from the complaining suppliers during my first months at the hotel and not the first weeks. Some of the complaints had been by phone and I had asked them to write.

As I scrolled down I found a whole row of emails that appeared in blue. When you open and read the email, it turns black, and I fought a moment of panic. Sometime last month, I had ignored a whole bunch of mails that could have been important. Then I remembered. There had been a group of businessmen from Germany, and with my schoolgirl Deutsch, I had won them over. Each one had promised that he would soon be back and would book with us, and one day, all of these mails had come in. By reading the first line preview, I could see that they were the promised bookings and I had forwarded them to the reservation department with a request that they add regards from me to the response. I should have erased them as soon as the bookings were made and I proceeded to do so, until I came to the next to last one. It was not from Germany, but from the hotel, and I had missed it because it was hidden from me by my own carelessness. It was from Marshall. I hesitated. What would I find in this message from the dead? What I found had me speechless.

'I know what you did, and I have witnesses. You took bribes and now I want my share. I will not be too greedy. Fifty dollars a week should be just right, in a sealed envelope in my mailbox. If you should be foolish enough not to pay, Mr. Hanley will be next on my mailing list and I have proof.'

Speechless? I was flabbergasted. He had tried to blackmail me and when, of course, I had not paid, he actually went to Hanley. I never would have paid, but if I had gotten the mail, I could have gone to Hanley myself. Someone who really had it in for me had given Marshall false information, and Marshall, more of a creep than I had imagined, had thought that he could profit from it. I had to find those letters.

I may not be a child of the digital generation, but I had certainly come of career age into it. My first instinct had been to look in the computer, but what if the letters were paper. There had been a time when people actually wrote a letter on paper, put it in an envelope, stamped it, and mailed it. Official files were in Milly's office, but all of the reports and pending files were in mine, and I started to look.

There were two piles of 'it can wait until tomorrow' papers. One was on the corner of the desk and one was in a drawer. After telling myself that there was no way I could have left letters in that pile for over a year, I admitted that it was indeed sadly possible. Opening the drawer, I pulled out a stack of papers and began to go through them. A lot went into the wastebasket, and some of them were months old, but there were no letters of complaint from the suppliers. Just in case, I would check again after looking at the ring binders in the low birchwood bookcase behind my desk. My files on Food and

Beverage were the first to be checked, with no result, and some of the older pages came out of the binder to be checked again. The files on purchasing mainly included price quotations, but to eliminate the possibility that I has misfiled, they joined the growing stacks of paper. In no time, my desk was covered with files of various colors. There were files on the floor, and files on the two guest chairs, and the filing cabinet was empty. At that very minute, Milly tapped on the door and without waiting for the 'Not now please' that stuck in my throat, walked in. She looked around amazed.

"I gather that you are looking for something."

"Yeah, and not finding it."

"What are you looking for? Maybe I can help."

"When we first came here, I got letters of complaints from some of the F and B suppliers. I need those letters, but I can't find them."

"I came in to remind you to go to lunch. You said that you wanted to eat in the restaurant with the convention guests to get a feel on how it's going. You go to lunch. I'll clean up here, and if those letters exist, I'll find them."

I couldn't refuse. She knew that I almost always tried to eat with guests to get a feel of how the food was and to snoop on conversations about their accommodations, the service they were getting and anything else they might praise or denigrate. It was the best kind of feedback, because they had no reason to lie, maybe just to exaggerate a bit. I didn't want

Milly or anyone else to sense my desperation, and if I decided not to go, she would be very suspicious. She would wonder how important those letters could be. It all had to seem casual. She was never a gossip, but I did not want her doubting my motivation.

So I smiled and thanked her and walked down the stairs from our office mezzanine floor to the main dining room on the lobby level. I could never enter that room without a smile of pleasure. The previous owners had been so good at reconstructing the hotel and had given it truly beautiful rooms and banquet halls, but they had been so bad at running it that they had lost this Boston treasure. This dining room was one of the gems that they had created. Dark red velvet drapes edged but did not cover the ceiling-high windows with a narrow sill that was low enough for seated diners to look out at the Charles River and watch the sailboats skimming over the sun-sparkled water. The white and blue paneled walls and the ceiling with a bas relief rosette in the center, gleamed in the bright light, and the dark wood tables and waiters' stations shone with polish. The chairs were upholstered in blue and red stripes. For lunch, we usually set with placemats, but in honor of the convention, crisp cream linen covered the table tops in the section of the dining room closest to the windows, where many of the convention guests were already seated. The buffet which divided the room in half was laden with salads and vegetables and hot plates with fish and meat. Guests lined up at the station where a cook in white jacket and toque sliced from a turkey on one side of the carving board and prime rib on the other. I took a green salad and began to search for an available table when I was jostled. I turned around and saw a blond head and freckled neck. The guest turned to apologize, turned bright red, dropped several pieces of asparagus on the carpet and began to stammer.

I winced and smiled. "It's all right Mr. Riley. Please enjoy your meal."

He turned away before he could see my choked giggle. I bent down to pick up the asparagus and glimpsed Betsy waving at me as she approached.

"What was that all about?"

"I last saw that gentleman early this morning when he was locked out of his room. It was the wrong room, he was drunk, and he wasn't wearing much more than those freckles."

She chortled and I had a vain hope that I would be able to eat without getting the third degree, but she wasted no time and got right into it.

"May I join you? I need to talk with you. Mom doesn't say that you'll be wanting to talk with me when she's intending that we talk about the weather." She paused. "Well?"

"I can't. It's for your sake. I would have to swear you to secrecy, and you wouldn't be able to do that."

"Are you solving your problem without help?"

"Not really."

"Okay, then spill it."

"You can't tell anyone. Not yet."

"All right."

"It's not all right, but here goes. When we came here, things were in a shambles."

"I remember that. Hanley had me come in to do a bit of spying even before he decided to buy. I got a job in security, and even I was appalled. He grilled me for hours before he decided that what was wrong could be fixed." Interested in my story, but also hungry, she began to sip soup. If she was so casual, maybe a light version would do.

"A week or so after I started I began to get phone calls and letters from suppliers saying that the low bids never got the order, and since I was new, could I please look into it. I didn't have to look into anything to know that what it meant was kickbacks. Hanley asked me not to do any wholesale firing, so I gave instructions about new buying policy to the chef, and he seemed to buy into it. I even thought that I caught a glimpse of relief."

"If this is the big secret, Hanley knew all about it."

"No, that's just the beginning, because now I think that it wasn't the chef. I really tromped on somebody's toes and he's been resenting it ever since. I am positive that the chef is cool. We get along too well and he's not that great an actor. So there's someone else who is mad at me and wants revenge, and found a way to get it."

"How?"

"I was being blackmailed, but I didn't know about it because the letter went astray."

"I don't get it."

"Actually I was the one who didn't get it. It wasn't really a letter. It was an email and I sort of misfiled it without reading it. I thought it was something else."

"I gather that you found the mail. What did it say?"

"Someone told someone else a lie, that I was the one getting kickbacks, and the someone else believed him and decided to blackmail me, but I didn't get the letter so he went to Hanley,"

"You are really confusing me. Why don't you just confront the someone in front of Hanley?"

"Not possible. Hanley is away for almost two weeks."

"So wait until he gets back." She stared at me, realizing that I had left something out.

"And what else is chewing you up."

"It was Marshall." I sighed a deep sorrowful sigh. "I did not kill him, I swear, but when I saw that email, I could have killed him except that someone else already did."

She choked and soup sputtered all over the table. Wiping her mouth and the tablecloth with her napkin, she stared at me. I could see how quickly she understood my dilemma.

"Peter."

I nodded.

"You're right. I can't lie to him. But I don't have to volunteer anything. I doubt he'll even question me, except unofficially and very generally. Don't worry. We'll handle that if and when we have to. Now, how can I help?"

"I'm not sure."

"Well, let's look at your list of suspects."

"Um."

"You don't have a list of suspects? The most important way to help you is to find the person who killed him. You really do need my help."

"That's what your mother said."

"My mother is usually right."

"I mean about finding the killer."

"That, too." She looked at me and shook her head sadly. "There is a good side to the blackmail, you know. If he tried to blackmail you, it probably wasn't his first time, so maybe what we're looking for is someone else he blackmailed. That could be a powerful motive for murder."

I suddenly felt that there was a way out if this mess. I had been feeling conquered, hopeless, and very unlike myself. I am usually so much in control and I was faced with a situation that I couldn't control and a problem that I couldn't solve.

My brain had been suffering from a sort of virtual concussion, but it was now beginning to work again.

"The odds are that it was someone from the hotel, because he knew about the trap door."

Betsy nodded. "You're right. It could be anyone at all who had heard about the trap door, but we can't suspect everyone. That will get us nowhere. We have to narrow it down, so, it was most likely someone who works or worked in reception. If that doesn't work out we can widen the search. We shouldn't talk here. You never know who might be listening."

I looked around us at the mob lining up at the buffet or sitting and munching. There were a lot of people, but they were all wearing convention badges. "You could be right, but I doubt it. What I see around us is a bunch of inebriate guests who are having lunch instead of a late breakfast. Anyway, the best way to hide is in full view. On the other hand, I think we should eat something and then make plans."

Betsy, who was always fit and thin despite never refusing food, agreed and joined the line for prime rib, where she loaded up. I had little appetite and had taken a selection of salads with just enough steamed salmon to qualify as protein. I figured a cup of rice pudding would finish my food pyramid as the carbohydrate in the equation, and began to munch. Betsy returned and, looking at my plate of rabbit food accompanied by a pale dessert, wrinkled her nose, but kept her silence. I guessed that she was feeling too sorry for me to berate me for not eating enough.

As I munched, I thought about the favorite subject of an introvert. Me, myself, and what was wrong now. I never quailed at the need to criticize myself and being honest, I knew that I had lost all semblance of control. But, in the midst of introspection, I felt that I was getting myself back together again. I hated losing control. As a teenager, that had been my real reason for refusing to indulge in grass, when everyone else was experimenting. I tried once, started to giggle wildly and even in a haze knew that I was finished with the experiment. I knew the source of this fear, too. I had learned to keep constant control from my mother. Except for one extraordinary time, I had never seen her lose control, but for me it was not emulation, it was keeping her at bay. She was a constant fount of criticism and for her I had to be the smartest, the prettiest, the best dressed, and the most popular. Early on, it became obvious to me that I couldn't really do it all, but I could keep control so that it would seem that, at least I was trying. Truthfully, I learned early on that I could make her think that I was the smartest, but the rest was out of the question so I learned to put on a show for her.

That probably was why I had been attracted to the hotel business. First of all, it was really a business that required brains for success, but it was also theater. Everything was all in perception and a large part of the job was putting on a show for the guests. After all, these guests all had beds and food at home. We had to give them something more. We had to provide them with an experience that would make them want to return to us again.

Well, if perception was everything, I would have to create the perception that I was innocent, and I didn't have a lot of time to do it. I knew something about Marshall that might lead to a clue. Could I trust Betsy enough to tell her about it? I decided to wait. My fear that she would be unable to keep my secret from Peter was real.

"After we eat, it would help if you try to get a list of all the people who ever worked here in reception. Then we can start trying to trace them"

"It would be a lot easier if Peter could help."

"No!" I yelped.

"Okay, okay. I'll do it. What about you?"

"I'm going to have to start worrying about perception, and do what I should have done already."

She looked at me with puzzlement. "What are you talking about?"

"Remember, our reception manager was murdered and we also have a massive headache of a convention going on. The staff is going to need some help tender loving care if we want them to survive this week. It's my job to make sure they get it."

Betsy made a funny face, nodded and rushed off.

I headed back for my office. I could have called Milly to tell her that I would be wandering the various departments but I was hoping that perhaps she had found something. I walked into the outer office and found that all the files that I had strewn about were neatly stacked on her cabinet in a tower that was a yard high. She was holding a page in a plastic sleeve and chuckling.

"What's so funny?"

"I only found one letter. I guess you kept it because it was so cute."

I held out my hand to take the letter which was handwritten on a pale yellow page lined in light blue and obviously torn out from a notebook.

"Come on. I found it. Let me read it to you."

Reluctantly I nodded.

"'Dear Missus Bar. I was very happy to know that you would be the GM at the Treasure because I got to know you so well when you were at the Mall.'"

"He knew me so well that he didn't even remember my name right."

"He doesn't spell so great either, but I'm just getting to the good parts. Ahem. 'At the Mall you drove a hard 'bargenn', but you were always fare.' Did you do the purchasing there?"

"No, Milly, I never did the purchasing there as you well know, and I am, of course, always fair, but I never bargained with him. Every Christmas, he would bring me a bottle of grappa that I would open at our staff party. It was so powerful a relaxing tipple that half of the staff members were so relaxed they couldn't work the next day."

"So he was bribing you with expensive alcohol."

I looked at her sharply and she returned me a wide innocent smile.

"As for expensive, I always suspected that he made it himself."

"Anyway, on with his sad tale. 'I sell good produce, you know, but at the Treasure Hotel, no matter how low I quote, I never get the bid. Why is that? You have to know why. Now you are the big boss, so do something. You asked me to write, so I write. Thanks, Ignacio.' That's what you wanted to find, isn't it? Do we buy from him now?

"That's exactly the letter that I wanted to find. Too bad that there was only this one. As for giving him business, I sign the checks, so I remember seeing his name, but I don't do the buying here, I just set the guide lines."

"Don't be so touchy. Come on, smile, and you know you can trust me, so lighten up. It'll be okay. Also, speaking of signing checks, it is that time of the month."

"I'll do it, I promise, but not now. With everything in an uproar, I want to check around the departments to make sure everyone is happy, so later, huh?"

I curtsied, smiled, and thanked her for finding the letter. It went directly into my small office safe, but even added to my emailed instructions to the chef it might still not be enough.

CHAPTER NINE

Rebecca - Tuesday Noon

I decided to start with the housekeeping staff. Most of them barely knew Marshall, but the brunt of the extra work of the convention fell on them. As I wandered the corridors, I saw open doors where the rooms were unoccupied, and orphaned housekeeping carts parked along the way. I found them all sitting together in their office having a coffee break.

"Hi, boss-lady," Anna, the department manager, welcomed me. "Olga, make another cup of coffee. Marianna, scrunch over and make more room for Rebecca."

The old green velvet sofa that Anna had scrounged for her office already held four girls, but they squeezed over to let me in. We drank coffee, and I shared my story of the half naked guest locked out of his room. It turned out that I had been lucky to have met only one example. All morning, they had been dealing with naked men who were too drunk to be anything more than an annoyance. We all laughed. The irritation over the mess created by yesterday's bonfire had changed to humor. After all, it had been pretty funny. Anna had told half her staff to come to work later than usual, so that they would not waste time waiting for guests to leave their rooms, and they were all in a good mood despite the extra work. I had come down to their office to try to lift their spirits, and they had lifted mine. There are a lot of hotel people who work very hard and a lot of them work hard physically, but few work as hard as these women do for so little pay and with so much good cheer. They are a real melting pot. Tensions sometimes break out on the lines between the Puerto Ricans, the Russians, and the Chinese, but Anna was a master at repairing the damage and for this earned every penny of her salary.

Then Anna asked the question that I had expected. "What about Marshall. It was murder wasn't it? Everybody wants to know. Did the police catch the killer? Are we in danger? The girls are a bit nervous."

"We're all a bit nervous. The police are working on it and no one here should be worried. It's all under control." I turned to face them all. "I understand how you feel. I just want to request that you not talk about it where guests can hear. Okay?" They all nodded seriously.

"I'm going back into the fray. If you have any problems in one of the rooms that you can't handle, just let me know."

"Sure, but the only thing worrying me now is that I'm losing my memory. I used to be able to remember every single room, occupied, empty, arrival departure, but I keep on finding rooms that are marked 'dirty' that I could swear were marked clean before." She shook her head in self disparagement.

"Well, we're all getting older. Thank God for computers to keep us in line."

I hugged her and waved goodbye after extricating myself from the sofa, and headed for reception with a short detour to the engineering storeroom.

Visiting the maintenance department was more politics than anything else. Potter, whose name was really Piotr, a name mutilated by staff from various nationalities trying to say Piotr, certainly didn't need my help or advice. In fact, it was usually the opposite, but he was the elected union rep, and that made keeping him happy one of the most important things I did. Fortunately, I could keep him happy by dropping in with two cups of tea, one for me with milk and one for him with lemon and a few cubes of sugar like my father used to drink.

We sat and sipped our tea, with him drinking it noisily through the sugar cube held between his teeth. He sat at his desk in a sagging, dilapidated, leather chair on wheels and I perched on a stool at the work counter. The shelves on all the walls held small plastic containers, each filled with every imaginable assortment of nails, screws, nuts, bolts, small black electric connectors, plumbers' tapes, electrical tapes, and other items unidentifiable at least to me. The room was cozy and comfortable despite the utilitarian decor. Every time I walked in, it reminded me of my father's home workshop.

"What's the damage from the bonfire?"

"Just a few bucks for a melted outlet and some wire, but if you want me to, I can inflate that."

"No need to do that. Just give me an account of all the hours you put in fixing it all up, and I guarantee that will give those reps something to choke on when I put it on their bill. They'll try to charge their companies and I bet they'll have zero success. Serves them right."

"Just keep me in the loop about Marshall. My people are asking and I have to know what to tell them."

"No problem. Anyway no one's gunning for hoteliers at random as far as the cops know."

We laughed and then, as usual, I listened to his stories of places he had worked, in the States and in Mother Russia. Luckily for me, he was a real raconteur and, as usual, he soon had me laughing to the point of tears. The time passed so quickly that we were both surprised when his morning staff came in to finish their shift. I apologized and began to head towards reception, prepared to spend time waiting. Then I reconsidered.

Three o'clock in the afternoon was no time to chat with anybody. One shift was finishing up and briefing the evening shift just arriving. I decided to use the time doing something that I should do even though I didn't want to.

There was someone in the kitchen who seriously wanted to do me harm. In fact, he apparently wanted to do me serious harm. I didn't have any idea who it was, and in the kitchen, full of sharp knives, it was hard to watch your back. Usually I loved to visit there. When I did my first 'stage' in Switzerland, it was in the kitchen, but now I feared that I would feel totally ill at ease.

There were two ways to get into the kitchens, from the loading ramp at the beginning of the process where food and supplies came in, and from the restaurant area where the finished product came out. That sounds industrial, and it is, but it's more. Much, much, more. If there is the right kind of chef, it's an efficient industry mixed with art and passion. Does that show that I love the kitchen? It should, because I do. Today, I wasn't feeling that way at all.

I decided to walk outside the hotel, to swing around, and to come in through the ramp. It was late for deliveries and the driveway was empty except for the garbage compactor. The green monster that squatted off to the side was probably by far the least glamorous thing in any hotel. On a hot day, garbage stinks. The longer it stays, the more it stinks and the less the stewards who hose down the compactor want to be near it. I try to pay the area a visit every day or so, so that they know I'm watching, or sniffing, to be more accurate. So I sniffed and it wasn't too bad. Walking through the corridor, I looked at the gleaming refrigerator and freezer doors. Some of them have a second access on the ramp for deliveries and none of them held any cooked food. All the cooked food was already in gastronorm pans ready to be reheated before being served and they were in different refrigerators. At this hour, the evening meals were almost ready except for finishing touches. Good smells permeated the air. There were crisp salads, containers heaped with slices of roast beef, chicken, vegetables for chow-mein, and fried fish. Bright green raw asparagus and broccoli awaited a last minute blast of heat, and the sweet carrots and pineapple bits perfumed the air. The sand colored non-skid floor, which for sure had been carpeted with bits of food not long ago, had been cleaned. The white tiled walls sparkled in the light from the long strips of bright fluorescents in the ceiling.

I stood back and watched the chef checking each and every gastronorm pan, the standard sizes of pan used everywhere in the world for cooking and storing food. He was concentrating so hard on tasting, adding flavoring here and there, that he didn't notice me.

How well did I know this man? I realized, with some embarrassment, that I really didn't know him at all. At all our meetings together, we got along well. I thought that he respected me. Because I had studied in Europe, my training was heavily practical. I knew a lot about the culinary arts, and I made sure that he knew it. He would often consult with me about menus and I found it flattering, but what if he was doing this just to flatter the boss? I knew that he was married and had twins, but I couldn't remember how old or what sex. I didn't know him as a person. I knew him as a tool that operated perfectly in the complicated machinery that made up a central part of the hotel. I was probably going to need his help as a person and not as a tool and I didn't know how to get it.

I studied him as he worked. He was short, stocky and athletic, although I could see just the very beginning of a pot belly from frequent tasting of his own food. His light eyebrows were bushy and his dirty-blond somewhat curly hair was long enough to fringe the top of his collar. He worked with a spare efficiency of motion that was pleasing to watch. Like many chefs, he no longer wore spotless whites with black buttons, but was dressed entirely in black. Pants, chef's jacket, and neckerchief contrasted with clean white clogs. The hat he should have been wearing was nowhere in sight. I walked closer and he looked up and smiled. His dark brown eyes crinkled and I saw for the first time that he should have had orthodontia as a child.

"Looks good, Chef. I just wanted to tell you how happy the convention people are about the food."

"That's always nice to hear, but I thought that you didn't want to do anything to encourage them to come back."

I laughed. "I hope that doesn't mean you're going to spoil the food to make them go away, not that the sight of them going away wouldn't make my day."

It was his turn to laugh. "No seriously, I know that these guys know food from the hotels and restaurants where they work. Their compliments mean something, but I have the feeling that most of the time they're too drunk to even know what they're eating."

I looked around at the army of steel work tables. "I don't see any desserts. You figuring they'll leave before the meal is over?"

"Very funny. You know me better than that. Donny had a family party in Worcester. He asked to get off early enough to get there in time. Don't worry, all the pies and cakes are ready, and we've also got ice cream, so no one's sweet tooth will suffer. We both came in early to do the work."

"Chef, you are one good guy."

He ducked his head and murmured, "I really got to finish here. Thanks for coming down."

I had seen this man reduce his staff to trembling terror when they had screwed up, but now I was seeing the other side of a man who would blush at a compliment. Customary as it is to invite the chef out to applause after a banquet, this secretly shy man would do almost anything to avoid the encomium.

I smiled and walked away into the empty dining room. There hadn't been a sight of any of the cooks, but some of them could have been watching and listening from another room, and one of them wanted me ruined.

Half of the dining room was ready for breakfast next morning. The convention group would not be eating dinner there because they had a dinner outside the hotel, and the few other resident guests who might want dinner would be served at the lobby window bar, where they could be enchanted by the sights and light on the river while they ate. We often had outside guests, attracted by reports of great food, an extensive wine cellar, and an entrancing view. The banqueting department, knowing that the convention guests were away tonight, had taken several large group reservations for dinner. Thinking about it, I felt a bit jealous. It would have been so nice to be able to sit down to a meal, with no worries except what to order. The dining room was silent. The tables were covered in crisp white linen, the silverware gleamed, the crystal sparkled and the silent colonial white and blue room with the view of the river was a prima donna waiting for the curtain to rise.

I sighed. One brief moment of peace, and now reception awaited.

Jeri was standing over one of the newer girls, letting her do the handover of the morning to the evening shift all by herself, while making sure that nothing important was missed. 'Good girl,' I muttered to myself. Despite my pleas, Marshall had always held his authority close to himself, fearing to train more than the bare necessity, so that no one could threaten his superiority.

"Let's talk for a minute. We have no office to go to, but things are under control and we can go over to the bar."

She smiled wryly and clambered out of the reception area. The armchair had been replaced by a makeshift stage that she used with her usual grace. We walked to the huge window that overlooked the river, where small tables were scattered and a compact bar-coffee shop served guests. The waiter approached, but both of us waved him off.

"Jeri, how's it going?"

"All right, I guess, but it's embarrassing. Every time I find myself alone, I start to cry."

"That's not embarrassing. It's human."

She turned pink. "Is it terrible to say that I didn't even really like him? Despite that, I still burst into tears. I mean, I knew him, and I worked with him, and now he's dead, and not just dead but murdered. Do the rest of us have any reason to be afraid?"

"I don't think so. I hope not, at least not while the police are swarming all over the hotel, and by the time they finish, I hope they'll catch whoever did it. I bet it had something to with him personally, and not to the rest of us. He wasn't easy to like. I doubt that he had many friends here, even though he liked people calling him 'the Hammer'."

"I hope you're right, because all of the staff are very nervous. I dropped a file on the floor and Marlin almost jumped over the counter."

I could just imagine pudgy Marlin trying to escape over the reception counter. He was living proof that hotel uniforms are not designed with the weight-challenged in mind.

"What about guests?"

"If they even know about it. I wouldn't worry. No early checkouts. We are still stuck with them until Thursday, heaven help us."

I thought about my next step. Should I wait or not? On the one hand, Jeri deserved to know what I had in mind for her, and on the second, I didn't want her to get any ideas about leaving.

"Jeri, I know that this could wait, but we might as well get it over with."

She looked at me with wide eyes, and I realized that I was scaring her.

"I want you to take over here in reception."

"You mean until the chain appoints someone to succeed the Hammer?"

"The chain doesn't appoint, I do, and I want you to run Reception."

"Thank you, really, but maybe we should wait until things calm down. Also, just to make sure. This is really sudden."

"First, no. I don't think we should wait, because it's important to keep things as normal as possible. Second, I am sure. Lastly, it's not sudden. Marshall was already here when I came, and I had no reason to let him go, but from the beginning, I thought you were the better choice. I had every reason not to tell you, but I haven't changed my mind or doubted, even once."

"Oh, my god. I don't know what to say." Tears sprang up in her eyes.

"I'm not worried. You'll have plenty to say, the next time we disagree at the morning briefing. I'll notify the main office tomorrow, and we'll talk money after that."

"Money?"

"There's a substantial raise attached to the promotion. I just want to get their okay for the specifics."

Jeri, a single parent, who depended on her elderly mother for childcare, dissolved in tears.

"That's just not like me. I am sorry."

I hugged her. "I know, and congratulations." In fact, I was a little teary myself.

It was a good time to make my escape, and I headed for the office to check messages and the like. For about a half an hour, I buried myself in the office doing triage on all the messages and letters. I dealt with everything that was urgent, put aside anything that was important but could be put off and consigned most to the wastepaper basket. Just as I sighed in satisfaction, I heard two women shouting in Milly's outer office. I stuck my head out in time to see the retreating hourglass shaped back of a very angry and very sexy female. A cascade of yellow-blond curls streamed halfway down her back and a torrent of curses hung in the air as she stomped out. Her tight leopard print skirt was missing enough length to make another skirt and tight enough to show her panty line. The black blouse, seen from behind, was tight enough to strangle her. Her cork wedged heels were built up so high that she was in danger of falling on her face.

"What was that all about," I asked Milly, who was sitting at her desk, shocked to uncharacteristic pale silence.

"That was Marshall's wife."

"Marshall wasn't married. He didn't have a wife."

"Apparently he did, and she had the marriage certificate to prove it," she responded drily.

"What did she want?"

"She wanted all of the personal papers that she said he kept in his desk. I told her that we had no way to get to his desk and that she would have to talk to the police. That was not what she wanted to hear and she told me so in language that would stun a longshoreman. If he had to live with that, it's no wonder he was so awful."

"I didn't know that you didn't like him. You never gave a clue."

"You almost never gave a clue, but you didn't like him either."

Not bothering to deny it, I asked, "How did you know?"

"Whenever you had a meeting with him, your lip would curl as if you had just eaten something spoiled. Every single time. I know you so well, but I don't think it was obvious to the others."

The phone rang, and it was Jeri asking if I could come back to the lobby. I found her holding a pile of letters from one of the convention guests who wanted to leave early and get a refund. The special rate they paid was for a package, and the best that I could do was to charge him full rate for the number of nights that he wanted to stay. He wasn't going to like that, so I started to read all the correspondence back and forth just to make sure that no one had promised him anything. Jeri and I were discussing one of the early letters when she abruptly changed the subject.

"Betsy's boyfriend just walked in. Maybe you could ask him when we can get our office back. I really need the files for arrivals, especially if they're gonna be departures in a few days. Try, huh?" She placed her palms together in mock prayer.

I nodded. "I'll do my best." The files were in a closed cabinet behind Marshall's desk. There were always three ring binders, one was labeled 'Today', the next was 'Tomorrow', and the third was labeled with a red number three. These binders included all the information for arrivals. Of course, the facts were in the computer, as well, but there were vouchers, personal letters with special requests and the like, that had not been scanned and existed only in the missing binder. Unfortunately, 'Today' was already yesterday, and 'Tomorrow' was a today that was mostly gone. Jeri was understandably peeved at not having those files and so was I. They were in a closed cabinet, there was no chance of trace evidence on them, and the police had already checked them over. So, why not?

I smiled as sincerely and broadly as I could while I walked over to Pete who was talking to the receptionist. I tapped him on the shoulder and he whirled to face me.

"I was looking for you."

"That's a nice coincidence. I was looking for you. We have a small request about getting a few files out of the office."

"I hope we can release the crime scene in a few days. I'm really sorry, but nothing can go out of there until then."

"Pete, that's out of the proportion. Files in a closed cabinet can't possibly be a clue. Suppose we photocopy all the material under your supervision," I added hopefully.

He shook his head.

"I need to talk with you."

"Fine."

"Not here. At the station."

"Why?"

"Too many interruptions here. The station is better. After we finish, I'll give you a lift back. There's no need to take your car, and parking's a bitch there anyway."

I was liking this turn of events less and less, but I didn't see any choice, and I didn't want to argue with him. I called Milly to tell her what was happening, and that she could leave on time if I wasn't back. That was unusual enough. We walked out to the unmarked car standing right at the entrance, got in and drove away without another word from Peter. I was silent, too, but my mind was whirling.

CHAPTER TEN

Rebecca Tuesday Evening

Was this really just routine? Were we heading for the police station just to avoid interruptions? Had the police managed to track Hanley down, and had he told them about the blackmail? Had Betsy let something slip? Were they going to arrest me? While flooded by questions, I tried to maintain a calm face to give the impression that everything was cool with me.

The minutes flew, and we soon pulled up to the red brick station house. He was right. There was a lot of traffic and no parking, and Peter pulled around to the fenced-in parking lot behind the station. I expected that we would go in through the back entrance, but he surprised me. He shook his head and walked back around to the front.

"You don't want to go there. It's holding cells and locker-rooms."

I appreciated what seemed to be consideration, but I wasn't any too sure. I had been there often to pick Betsy up or drop her off when she first started living with Peter, but had rarely been inside and I looked around with curiosity. Well, I laughed to myself, cynically, there's a reception desk with a receptionist in uniform, just like a hotel, and even the decor was simple but pleasant. When we passed by the desk through a door next to it, the resemblance ended. Everything was institutional beige, the walls, the floor tiles and the ceiling. All the desks were metal and functional. Pete hustled me through a large room with a number of unoccupied desks pushed back to back and into a glassed in office with vertical blinds that he closed. There were a number of gold bordered certificates on the wall along with pictures of what had to be the captain and the mayor. There were also pictures on the large wooden desk, but they had been turned face down, and I assumed that they were family pictures kept private.

"This isn't like any interrogation room on TV, is it?"

"Why should we be in an interrogation room? In any case, with you, it's kid gloves all the way."

"Not that I mind, but why?"

"Because you have helped us in the past, and we don't forget, because the hotel is very generous when we sell tickets for the policemen's ball, and because Hanley is a very good friend of the mayor, not necessarily in that order."

He chuckled and I joined in, half-heartedly. Maybe it was a good sign that he was buttering me up, and maybe it was a bad one.

"Do you want something to drink? We have cold drinks and an actual real coffee machine that makes actual real good coffee."

My mouth was dry although I didn't really want to drink, but if hospitality delayed the inevitable, I was all for it. "Diet coke, if that's okay?"

He nodded, and left the room, returning quickly with two cokes. I realized that he was delaying as much as I was.

He sat down, not behind the desk, but in the second guest chair, facing me. He heaved a huge sigh.

"When did you arrive at the hotel yesterday?"

"A little before seven."

"Are you sure?"

"Of course I'm sure. There was a guest trying to check out, and shouting to beat the band, because no one was in reception. I took care of her, and only then did we try to get into the office. That's when we discovered Marshall."

"Who are we?"

"The doorman and I."

"But didn't you arrive at the hotel much earlier?"

"No, I did not, and what is this all about?"

"Rebecca, when people drive into the parking garage and the gate is closed, as it usually is, guests use the phone there to call reception. Staff members use their employee card. You used your card at five seventeen AM. That would have given you plenty of time to do lots of things."

"I didn't. That is, I did use the card to drive in and turn around and drive out. I forgot something at home, and I went there. I came back almost two hours later."

"Why did you have to go back home? What is it that you forgot?"

At this point, my level of panic was in superdrive and I blacked it out. I simply couldn't remember why I had returned home. It was going to sound awful, but I had no choice.

"I don't remember, it was so long ago."

"Indeed. Yesterday. Ah hah."

"Whatever you think, I never walked into the hotel until much later. I was not there and no one saw me there."

"Who would see you at that hour?"

"Security or reception."

"Reception? You mean Marshall?"

By now my thoughts were as jumbled as thoughts can be, and I stammered, "No, no, not Marshall. Whoever was on shift before him. I can't remember who, because I didn't see him and because the work schedule is posted in the office that you have closed off."

"We'll come back to that later. What kind of a relationship did you have with Marshall? He was a pretty important department head for you."

"I don't lie, Pete. He was a colleague, but I had very little or nothing to do with him outside the hotel, and he was not my favorite person. I hope that I didn't make that obvious enough for anyone to know."

"Did he know?"

"What do you mean?"

"Well, he was doing something friends don't do. He was blackmailing you."

Damn Betsy, I thought. She was sure that we needed Pete's help, and she went right ahead doing what I had asked, no, I had begged her not to do. If Marshall was my first victim, she would be my second. I was fuming, and the anger helped me focus.

"Peter, are you arresting me? Because if you are, just say so and read me my rights. Then I call my lawyer, and then I am out of here, because you have absolutely no reason to keep me here, no reason at all."

"Calm down. I am not arresting you. I do need answers to questions, but that's not an arrest. Please understand that." He held out his hand in boyish supplication and despite myself I laughed.

"Well, I can prove that I went home. We have security cams at the parking garage entrance, and I'm sure you'll see me drive in and out. In fact, there are so many security and traffic cams along the way, you could probably trace me all the way down Comm Ave, and then back again just before seven o'clock."

He stood up. "Wait here. I'm going to get someone to do just that. That should solve a lot of problems."

He walked out leaving the door open, as a sign of trust, I guess. After a few minutes, I followed, staying by the open door. I saw him bent over a computer screen while someone sitting at the desk made adjustments to what I hoped was the disc from our security cameras.

The door to the large room flew open dramatically and I realized that the situation had gotten to me and made me lightheaded, for storming towards Pete was an aubergine. I blinked and rubbed my eyes and the aubergine morphed into an even more amazing hallucination. Heading for the two men studying the computer, was Marloo Fleischer, dressed in an eggplant colored suit with a fitted jacket and a pleated skirt that fell just below her knees. She wore black patent heels, her face was professionally made up and her hair was gathered into a neat bun. Marloo was Bridget's neighbor, and I knew her because many years ago she had taught Bridget how to make strudel. The family loved it so much that the two friends would meet every few weeks in Bridget's kitchen to stretch the paper thin dough and to invent fanciful fillings. I had never seen Marloo dressed in anything other than scuffed loafers, faded baggy jeans, a tee-shirt advertising sentiments such as saving the whales and a scraggly bun of graying brown hair that escaped in tendrils waving around.

She reached Pete, screeched to a stop and began to berate him in her rich Hungarian accent. "Shame on you! You know that she never killed anybody. Where is my client?

He gaped and then involuntarily glanced at me.

"Ah! You have her in the captain's office. I can just hear him. Kid gloves, remember kid gloves. You can use my office."

She shifted gears and headed for me. I was also gaping while she actually pushed me inside the office and slammed the door.

"I don't think they bug the captain's office, but with these characters, who knows."

"Marloo, what are you doing here? You're not a lawyer."

"If you are afraid that I am not a real lawyer, ask them out there. They catch them and I let them go free. They do not much like me, but that is their problem. Your charming secretary called Betsy, and she called her mama, and she called me. That is why I am here. Now, I hope that you have not told them anything."

"Why? They didn't read me my rights. I am not under arrest."

"Not yet. When you are so-called invited to a police station, you must come with a lawyer, and say nothing unless the lawyer says yes."

"But don't you look guilty if you come with a lawyer?"

"You look stupid if you do not. Now tell me what they asked and what you said. To them you must tell nothing, but to me you must tell everything if you want me to help."

"Well, I've told Bridget everything, and Betsy too much, so what the hell."

"Thank goodness, you told Bridget, but I would like to hear from you."

"Pete asked about when I came to the hotel because I drove in early, around five, but I had to go home and came back around seven."

"Why?"

"Because I left the water running for the garden irrigation, and it tends to splash on our neighbors window when it's on too long, so I went back, and then ate something and drank coffee."

"Did you tell him that?"

"No, because I got flustered and I forgot."

"Thank goodness."

"Why? It helps me."

"No, my dear, it helps them. If you tell them, why you go home, they can start to look how to prove it not so. If they don't know then they don't know what to disprove."

"Marloo, Pete is my friend. He wouldn't do that to me."

"Yes, my dear. He would. It is his job and he would do it. He would even do it harder because he is your friend. " She sighed and shook her head. "Did he ask anything else, anything about the subject you discussed with your boss?"

"He knew that Marshall was trying to blackmail me, but I didn't know myself until Hanley told me."

"Did you talk about it with Peter?"

"No."

"Good. Now we go. I will take you back to your hotel and tomorrow we will meet and plan strategy, first thing in the morning. I will come to you so we can see where it all happened.

She rushed me out and as we passed Peter, I waved at him. He seemed to still be in shock, and to be truthful, so was I, but I was more optimistic than I had been since the meeting with Hanley.

Marloo drove the same way she talked, with Hungarian verve, and I closed my eyes every time we took a corner, undecided which was better, knowing that we were going to crash, and holding tight, or letting fate happen. When we pulled up in front of the hotel, I kissed her goodbye and scrambled out. I stuck my head through the window to thank her.

"Well, it's my job, so the thanks are appreciated, but not necessary. Also, Bridget requested my assistance and we are good friends. We have a good 'barátság', a good 'Freundschaft', and that is very important to me, so maybe it is Bridget you must thank. She peeled off and I, shakily, walked into the lobby.

CHAPTER ELEVEN

Rebecca - Tuesday Night and Wednesday Morning

The barman was there, and the doorman, and two receptionists, and a housekeeper polishing handrails. Potter was there fixing a leg on an armchair that had not survived a drunken onslaught, and Betsy, with her bag over her shoulder, on her way home, and all stood there watching me arrive.

I smiled, walked behind reception, carefully removed the crime scene tape on the door to the office, put on booties from the pile that was still at the door, picked out one rubber glove and put it on my right hand, walked in, opened the cabinet behind the desk, and took out the three binders. I walked out, replacing the booties, glove, and the crime scene tape and presented the files to the receptionist. There was a moment of silence and then they all applauded and cheered.

I walked up to Betsy, shook my finger at her wordlessly and headed in the direction of my office. I was so angry at her that I didn't trust myself to talk. I was angry, but I also understood why she couldn't withstand the opposing pulls on her conscience. She loved Peter and he was a policeman. I think she loved me, too, but it wasn't the same. It couldn't be. This was what I had feared and was the reason that I hadn't wanted to tell her anything. If I told her how angry I was and how betrayed I felt, it could cut our friendship apart. So I kept quiet.

It would have been easier and nicer to do what I planned the way we once did things. Together. That was not to be. Maybe that was never to be again. I changed direction and headed for the human resource office.

Patsy's ditsy assistant was long gone and I needed the computer there. Patsy was our resident computer guru, and when she went on maternity leave, there was no way that she could let her so-called assistant handle the computer supervision. When we talked about the dilemma, I suggested myself.

"You?" She guffawed. "You barely know how to turn the computer on."

"Not funny and not true. I'm no expert, but I know enough to be the administrator and that's what I need now. Next to you I'm probably the most computer literate person here, and the company is always on line."

We agreed to make as few changes as possible. The codes would remain in her computer, and if I hit a problem I couldn't solve I would consult with her before any drastic move.

I needed the computer to get access to Marshall's program files because it was the only one with a list of everyone's password and logon name.

Marshall used to do something with his computer that no one knew about except me. I found out and I didn't call him on it or even tell him that I knew, because I thought that it might actually be a good idea. He used to spy on his staff. That sounds worse than it actually was and it sounds bad that I thought that it might be a good thing. But, actually it depended on why he did it. He didn't sneak around behind doors. He checked up on them through the computer. He would go into the program files and check on how they did registrations, and how long it took and how they allocated rooms and a lot of other stuff. Then they would get a compliment or a critique that would come out of left field. They had no idea how he knew. I don't think any of them ever figured it out, but it often had a good effect on performance because it made them extra careful the next time. If Marshall did make a habit of blackmail, this could be one way to get his information.

I could get to use his logon because I could get that from Patsy's computer. I couldn't use his computer because the police have it, but it would be as if I was looking at his own computer. I blessed the wonders of technology and got to work.

Opening the program with his logon, I fiddled around, pressing icons randomly, and within a minute I located the program that listed his recent actions on the computer. Now that I had it, I could go back in time and start with the beginning of his work as reception manager. Before then, he wouldn't have had the ability to snoop. It was weird. I was tracing a dead man just as if his dead fingers were pressing the keys.

To get comfortable with the program, I started with the files that he had created during the past few days. To my shock, I could see that he had changed the status of clean rooms to dirty, and not once, but for several rooms. If we allowed a potential guest to see a room and before we could stop him, he sat on the bed, rumpled it, used the toilet and washed his hands, we would have to send a room cleaner in to straighten the room again. Such a clean room could be marked dirty. If a maintenance man fixed something and made a mess, the clean room would be marked dirty. When a receptionist marked a room dirty in the middle of the night, without a check-in, the reason usually was someone using the room illegally. There were half a dozen ways to comp a room, to give it without charge. I could do it without giving a reason. So could Hanley. We comped rooms for travel agents, and for staff of other hotels in the chain if their manager requested, and for the other managers themselves. We comped rooms if that was the last resort for a severely offended guest. Every single one of these cases was reported on a blue form that landed on my desk. Always.

Okay, so he was not just a blackmailer. He was also a thief. That may sound overly dramatic, but the person using a hotel room illegally was stealing from Hanley. The police were prepared to call it theft, albeit reluctantly, and so were the courts. The thing is, that it usually never got to them. We would handle it ourselves, but there was no way to handle it with a dead man. Since Betsy had started to work as the head of security in the hotel, this never happened, or so I thought. It never happened because she had made sure that the night rounds included a random check of empty rooms, but the head of reception could prevent it if he told them to skip a room. He could do that once or twice. If he did it more often, it would get noticed.

I put it aside. When I had more information, I could try to fit the strangely shaped piece into the puzzle.

I wasn't sure exactly what I was trying to find. I was looking for anything that seemed suspicious, but if I searched every single file that he had ever created, it could take weeks. I had to narrow it down. I decided to look at the time period between Marshall's appointment as manager to the time that I arrived. The date that he began was in his personal file and the personnel files were in a locked filing cabinet. That lock was one of the few in the hotel to which I did not have the key. If I broke in obviously, it would lead to a real mess in the morning. Patsy's assistant, whose name I could never remember, was probably not dumb enough to miss signs of a break-in, although even that wasn't a sure thing. The cabinet was locked, but the lock was a standard file cabinet cheap inefficient version. I tried sharply tipping the cabinet half over, and to my delight, that worked. All of the four drawers came flying out. Skimming quickly through the H's, I found that Marshall had been working at the hotel since it opened, and had been made manager of the department two years later. That gave me seven years to search and I gagged in despair.

I had to learn how to play the system as quickly as possible. I knew how to do a lot of stuff, but spying was not one of them. I began to stress out until I realized that I wasn't actually doing anything that I didn't do when I wanted to check back on things that I myself had done on my computer. I wasn't spying on a different computer, I was using Marshall's login as if it were my own.

The computer was turned on. All I had to do was open the property management program using Marshall's username and password and I was in. Just to get a feel of it, I began to look at all the activities of the day before yesterday, Marshall's very last day. At first I looked at everything. There were all the normal activities of a fairly quiet Sunday afternoon. Some late guests were checked out. Rooms were blocked for the group that was to arrive, walk-ins were registered, a few guests were checked in and a few accounts were corrected. Whoa. Any account corrected had to be reported and the report should have been on my desk. Maybe, just maybe, the report was still on Marshall's desk waiting for the police to release it back to us.

I looked at the day before. This time I only looked at changes, corrections and amendments. It all looked normal. Then I searched Friday, and there it was again. Accounts corrected. There were a lot of accounts, some had amounts added and some had subtractions. These changes should definitely have been on my desk. They had one thing in common. All of them were accounts prepared by Lydia Stumble, our newest, least successful recruit to the reception department and most aptly named. She was sweet and welcoming to the guests, but she made mistakes every time she touched the computer. I had already talked about her with Marshall and suggested that we try Lydia out as a hostess in the dining room. Marshall suggested that we give her another chance, and it did seem that she was improving. Now all that had become clear. The question was what she was paying. I knew that she certainly had no money. That would have to wait. I had no doubt that she was not the killer. To find the murderer I would have to dig deeper and farther back in time, so I began the tedious task of checking every single change made by Marshall from the first day that he managed the department. I began to see double, and at some point I decided to print out every single change. In no time I had accumulated a foot high pile of paper. I searched and searched and searched, but found no red flags, except for a few other instances of massive corrections for someone who must have been like Lydia, new and unaccomplished, and female. They never covered a long period of time.

This was a sort of a possible clue. Maybe one of them wanted some kind of revenge for whatever he had taken as his price for silence. The more I thought about it, the more possible it looked. I noted the names of the receptionists that Marshall had protected. Then I decided that the time had come to try the spying app that Marshall used. To be more accurate, I had to find a way to see when Marshall had used the app. I didn't know how to do it. I spent too much time clicking randomly on every icon and then clicking on various combinations. This way was dumb and there had to be a better solution.

Nothing worked. I was probably far too tired to be effective. There had to be some way to find out how to do it. I looked at my watch. Three fifteen in the much too early morning, for crying out loud. What happened if a receptionist, almost all alone in the hotel, needed technical help with the computer program in the middle of the night? I gritted my teeth in frustration. How could I possible find a killer in this digital mess if I couldn't even remember that we had twenty-four hour service for the property management program? I called reception to ask for the number, and despite the hour, a bright cheery voice answered.

"Good Morning, Lydia speaking. How may I help you?"

Lydia? I wouldn't have to delay my questions for very long after all.

"Good morning, Lydia. This is Rebecca Bauer. Could you please give me the emergency number for the PMS technical assistance people?"

"Of course. Here you go. It's 11 91 11 3468912.

"Isn't that a foreign number?"

"Yes, ma'am. It's in New Delhi."

"Wow. Thanks."

"My pleasure, ma'am."

We go to India to get software help that we can't provide for ourselves. What kind of conclusions should I draw from that? It is an interesting thought, but I will have to think it when I have more time.

Dialing the number led to a bunch of recorded security questions to prove that I was really who I was. After answering a robot that left me amazed and a bit fazed at what technology could do, I was finally able to talk to a real human being. Finally, I got the help I needed from a gentleman who spoke a very British English with an Indian accent. There was no way to set a search that would show use of the spy app. I would have set a more general search that would include it. Did I also want to learn how to use the app itself or did I just want to trace its use?

I answered this question with a resounding yes, and he began to explain. He told me that the app did its job, but it wasn't easy or intuitive to use. He was patient and encouraged me to try while he was still on the line. I asked him for a minute's more patience so that I could write the directions down. I had no doubt that by tomorrow I would forget part of them, and the app seemed to be extremely useful. Of course I had only the purest intentions, unlike Marshall and his spying for profit. Seriously, the company had created a means of checking on the work of subordinates without their knowing and it was limited to their work product. It was meant to be a way of preventing the damage that Lydia, and those like her, could do. Unfortunately, if you put a tool in the hands of a thief, he would find a way to use it to steal.

Now, it was my turn. I started with the date that Marshall became the department head, the day that the system administrator had added his name to the list of people who had permission to do almost anything in the system. Looking for the sign of the spy app, I found nothing. Day after day, week after week, I found nothing. Almost ten months into the search, there was still no sign, and I decided to check out one more month and call my Indian friend again. Maybe I had misunderstood the way to identify the use of the app. Marshall had begun to manage the department in January, and in the end of November, possibly on an evening that was quiet and boring, he had decided to play with a new toy. He had spied on the morning shift. From that time on, he used the spy app every week, once or twice. I decided to print out the results from those days, so that I would have all the data when I wanted to get more details.

I remembered the days when our printers were pin printers. The pages were all connected and fell out of the printer in a continuous fold. It could be annoying to separate out one page, but at least the pages ended up in an organized neat pile. Now, with so many pages, the first time I let them pile up, there was no more room and the printer started to shoot them onto the floor. I ran to grab them and keep them in order while they continued to spill over. I made a grab for the pile still in the printer and realized that if I didn't stop the avalanche I would be left with a mess of data that I would have to reorganize. I stopped the flow, and breathed a sigh of relief. Adrenaline was keeping my body wide awake, but my brain was beginning to enter a state of confusion. It was time for coffee.

Patsy had left her coffee machine and a supply of Nespresso capsules for the staff to use while she was on maternity leave. There was a small pitcher of milk in an office size fridge and mugs on a shelf, each with a name painted on it. I took Patsy's, ran the fragrant hot coffee into it, spilled in a dash of milk and sipped with pleasure. It was four o'clock. I would work for another half hour, force myself to stop, take a room, and then force myself to sleep for a few hours so that I would not be totally useless during the day.

I had to try to analyze what had been going on. According to the files, Marshall had been spying randomly. He never did it more than once at a time, and almost never on the same receptionist twice in a row. A year later, that changed. He spied almost every night, and it was almost always the same person. The username that appeared over and over was ANDYP. Who was ANDYP and what was he doing that made Marshall want to spy on him. Second question first. I would have to do some spying of my own.

I took out the instructions that I had scrawled and began to check on whatever ANDYP was doing. ANDYP worked the evening shift five nights a week and almost never worked any other shift. On his eight hours from three to eleven, he spent his time doing all the things he should have been doing. He checked guests in, took some reservations and altered others during the hours when the reservation office was closed, made the charges in guest bills that were not automatic, and every few days he changed the status of a room from clean to dirty. That was the one thing he should not have been doing. There are a few legitimate reasons to mark a clean room as dirty, but they don't happen very often. If a 'walk-in', a guest who didn't reserve in advance but just walked in off the street, asked for a room, without breakfast, and paid in cash in advance, there was a right way to handle the reservation. There was also a crooked way, and ANDYP apparently favored it. He could take the money, give the guest a key, and mark a clean room as dirty so that it would be cleaned the next day. He would not check the guest in. The money would go into his pocket and if the night security officer would ask for a list of empty rooms, that room would be crossed off the list. It was almost foolproof then, and even today it could work. Betsy had taught her staff to print out the list of empty rooms and to check them, but a reception could still make up a good story. That would be enough as long as it was not too often. Then, ANDYP did it every time there was a walk-in. I could hear him offering a discount for cash. I boiled in anger. He was a thief and possibly a murderer, and he had worked here. Marshall had known and he had done nothing. Worse, he had apparently taken a cut. I gritted my teeth and fisted my hands. If only I had him here in front of me. I would teach him a lesson or two.

Now, I would have to check the files, to find out who it was. The filing cabinet I had ravaged earlier had a section for staff that had been fired or had left on their own. I guessed that the first name was Andy or Andrew or something like that, and the family name began with 'p'. There were a few 'p's but none matched. I knew that the personnel files were also computerized, but I had no idea how to look for them. Even Patsy's assistant knew how, but I didn't. At this hour, another call to India was out. There would be someone there to help, but I was running out of time. Whoever he was, I would find him, but as much as it irritated me, it would have to be later.

I badly needed to sleep and I needed a room. That meant that I would have to talk with the receptionist who just happened to be Lydia. Here was my chance to question her, subtly of course.

Just as in many hotels, the human resource office is deep in the bowels of the building, where guests do not trod. For many new employees, an interview here is their first chance to find out that the hotel business is not just glamour, elegant suites, crisp napery, uniformed staff and gleaming silver. Hotels hide away the steamy laundry, the smelly garbage, the dusty carpentry, and the files and staff arguments. There are no windows and no fresh air and I felt stifled after so many hours in what felt like an underground cave. The staff elevator took me to the lobby floor and with a wave to Lydia who seemed surprised that I was still here, I opened the main door and headed outside to breathe.

The cool night held only the barest of hints of the warmth of the day. The whoosh of traffic on Storrow Drive along the river and on Beacon Street a block away had dwindled to a whisper, and the noise and pollution were replaced by a whiff of lilacs planted next door. The streets were empty and I imagined that I could hear the sounds of the river. For the moment, this was where I was, and then I was back.

Lydia sat under the lights of the reception desk, reading a book that she had hurriedly hidden when I passed by. As long as the night shift work got done, there was never a problem with reading. Far better that she read than fall asleep. The shift was long and could be boring. In darkness, I was invisible to her and I studied her, wondering why we had hired her.

Most of the receptionists were attractive men and women, but it was not intentional. It couldn't be according to the law, and she was the proof that we obeyed the law. A stiff mousy brown pageboy straight out of the past did not cover a very high forehead. Her face was squarish, her lips were too full, her eyes too small, her nose too upturned, and she hadn't even the slightest idea of how to use makeup. All this sat on a drop-dead gorgeous knockout body.

Hotel uniforms have been designed for impossibly slim figures. Lydia's uniform disguised her and made her look chubby, even dumpy. Until this moment when, thinking that she was alone, she removed the jacket and stretched, she appeared to be nondescript. Until this moment, I could not even begin to guess what Marshall could have wanted from her. Now, with newly cynical eyes, it was crystal clear. The only question that remained was whether or not she had enough reason and sufficient will to kill him.

With her charm and warmth, she was beloved by the guests until their last day when she would screw up their bill. She could be the kind of person that makes a hotel better, but not in reception. If Lydia would agree to the suggestion that she become a hostess in the dining room, one of the cosmetic companies that used our suites for promotions would be bullied into a makeover for her. If she refused the offer, it was only a matter of a very short time before she would be fired. All that, of course, if she was not a murderer.

The door was locked. Of course. At this hour there was no doorman and no bellboy. The security officer making his rounds would be pressed into service to handle suitcases, if we got a last minute booking through the airport hotel phone. Hearing me ring, Lydia put her book down, put on her jacket, and pressed the button that would open the door.

"Thanks, Lydia, I really needed the chance to breath real air."

"When you went out, I thought you were leaving."

"No, I have to be here pretty early tomorrow, I mean today, so I'll take a room. Do we have one that's empty?"

"The presidential suite is available, or do you want something smaller."

"Definitely smaller. The hotel doesn't have to make an impression on me, and the cleaner works double to clean a suite."

"Oh. I'm sorry. I didn't think."

She was already flustered, blushing slightly, and she hadn't even made a real mistake yet. I asked myself again how we ever hired her.

Trying to get her to relax, I asked casually, "What are you reading? Is it good?"

"Oh, it's not a book, it's a notebook. I've been having a few problems with understanding sales tax, and Jeri asked me to make a list of taxes paid today. She told me how to use the special function on the calculator but every time I check it with my arithmetic it comes out different, so something is wrong with the calculator."

"Do you mind if I look? Maybe I could help." I held out my hand for the notebook.

She opened the notebook to a page with rows of calculations. Even with a glance, I could see her mistake. I sighed because Boston hotel tax is complicated, and it's even higher for a hotel with convention facilities, but her mistake had nothing at all to do with that.

"You've got the total tax absolutely right, but you're subtracting it from the total instead of adding it to the base rate." She looked at me wide eyed as if I was speaking a foreign language.

"I'll try to simplify. If the price was a hundred dollars, and the tax was ten percent instead of the real fourteen forty-five, what would the total be?"

She smiled happily. "A hundred and ten."

"If you start from the hundred and ten to figure out how much the base price was, you can't subtract ten percent. That would get you ninety-nine. You'd have to divide by..."

I looked at her and saw that I had already lost her. She was confused and looked wildly back and forth to the pages of the notebook and to me.

"Never mind. It doesn't really matter as long as you use the calculator the way that Jeri showed you. So just take it easy. Umm. Some time ago, you were offered a chance to work in the dining room. Have you been thinking about it?"

She blushed again and stammered, "It was because I was making a lot of mistakes, but I talked it over with Marshall. He helped me a lot and there aren't many mistakes any more. Now he's gone so I don't know how it will be." Tears filled her eyes.

Determined not to let this become a mourning session, I plowed on relentlessly. "This is really a good chance for you, and you should have no doubt that you are making mistakes again. It's not a crime, but for this job you need to be a little more comfortable with math than you are.

"I am afraid that Marshall didn't help you learn to avoid the mistakes. He covered for you and that could have been risky for him. Why did he do that? Did he ask something from you in return? I have to ask. Did he ask for favors that were sexual?"

She turned beet red and began to cry. I was afraid that I had blown my chance. I certainly hadn't been subtle and she had been an easy target.

"I can't tell you."

"You have to tell me."

"It wasn't like that. He helped me because he loved me. He didn't force me to do anything. It was totally innocent. I never met with him outside of work. He said that it would be improper."

I looked at her with a puzzled expression on my face that she misunderstood.

"You're thinking of sex, of intercourse." She whispered the words. "I never. He never."

She was silent, and a smile crept across her face as remembered. I did my best to maintain a noncommittal expression. Waiting for her to speak, I hoped that she hadn't completely shut down. The wait was worth it, because after a few minutes she answered. She finally had a chance to tell someone what had occupied her thoughts for so long, and the floodgate was open.

"I did an invoice for one of our returning guests and I totally messed it up. He was in a hurry, and he was annoyed. No. He was furious, and he started to yell. Marshall was in his office, and he rushed out, apologizing all the way. In seconds, he fixed the invoice, and after glaring at me, the guest stomped out.

"I started to cry, and Marshall led me into his office and held me while I cried. He held me for a long time, and it became, well it became something else. He began to open the top buttons of my blouse, and then he put his hand in and started to caress. I could see that he was getting hard. His bulge was thrusting at me, and I felt myself getting wet. Then he put his other hand up my skirt, but I was wearing panty hose, and then the bellboy knocked on the door. Marshall pulled away and I buttoned my blouse. That was that, and I thought that while it had been wonderful, it meant nothing. I was so embarrassed when I came on shift the next day. I was afraid to face him, but I was wrong. I was so wonderfully wrong. You see, we talked. He explained that we had to set limits because we worked together, but it was still love. Loving means caring. He would care for me and help me so that there would be no mistakes and he would be able to show his love with caresses." She reddened even more. "I bought a garter belt and regular stockings."

I swallowed. The poor kid thought that he loved her. I couldn't see her killing him. She still had no idea how much he had taken advantage of her innocence, and she had no idea that she should be angry.

I could scratch that possibility, but I couldn't leave her this way.

"You know that the guests really like you. They even come to spend time talking with you when they're in the lobby."

"I know," she answered with a smile. "I really love Boston history and I read a lot. There are so many good stories about places that you can walk to from here, so I tell them."

Hmm. There was no way to make her a concierge. She had no seniority, no knowledge of the ins and outs, and our chief concierge would kill me. I had to think of something fast.

"You know, if you take the hostess job, we can add a sort of club for families with children, and you could get time to tell them your stories. You would have to brush up on all the things that kids can do around here. That would be a win-win for you and for the hotel."

"I don't know what to say."

"Don't say anything. Just think about it. Okay?"

She nodded and turned to the key maker to prepare a key card for me. I took the key, left a few instructions for the morning shift, and staggered to my office to grab the emergency overnight bag that was always there and then to the elevator. These late hours were just not for me. I had long ago left that young age when midnight can be the middle of the day.

The key would not go into the lock, but after a few tries, the door opened. I know that I managed to get my clothes off, because when I finally woke up, I was wearing the t-shirt that I had borrowed from Jason for comfortable sleep and that I always left in the hotel along with a toothbrush and a few cosmetics, but I have no memory of it. Lydia had set a nine thirty wakeup call, and left a message to tell all the managers that the daily meeting would be an hour late. That would shock them. The nine o'clock hour for the meeting was holy, secretly because it was a way to ensure that the department managers would come to work on time. For once, I planned to be unconscious at nine o'clock.

The dream reincarnated the dead reception manager, but all his crimes had led him to be jailed. He looked out through the bars and began to yell wildly. Then he removed his shoe and began to bang with it on the bars. The clangor grew louder and louder and finally turned into insistent knocking.

Swimming up through the dream, barely awake, I climbed out of bed to answer the door. As I opened the door, Betsy stood there ready to pound again.

"Are you all right? They told me you were here, that you slept here. What's wrong?"

"What's wrong is that I just went to sleep after a night working to find our murderer. What's even more wrong is that before that I spent hours being grilled by your boyfriend who suspects me of murder because you couldn't keep your mouth closed. I'm going back to sleep, and the last person I want to see right now is you. If you want to skip the morning briefing, feel free"

She paled, began to speak, thought better of it and fled.

Then I slammed the door. Of course after that scene, it would be impossible to fall asleep. The next I knew, it was nine thirty and the phone was ringing.

CHAPTER TWELVE

Betsy - Tuesday Afternoon

Lunch with Rebecca had left me flabbergasted. I had no idea that she had managed to get herself in so much trouble, just by doing the right thing. When we parted, I wanted to run to my office and start searching through the files, sure that the right one would be obvious. Unfortunately, security in a big city hotel can be a lot of boring reports and hours with nothing much to do, mixed with emergencies and drama. Today's dramas ran the gamut.

The guest will always see it as an emergency whether he has left the hotel a week ago and just discovered that he forgot his jacket in the room, or when he returns from a day of business meetings minus his credit card. Both happened today and this is common enough for us to have solutions, but when someone's little three year old girl wanders out of her room and disappears into the maze of hundreds of almost identical rooms, this is a real emergency.

There are a lot of shelves and drawers in my office that are used only to store all the items that guests have forgotten. They are registered by date, room number and probable name, and they include everything from suitcases, cameras, eyeglasses, and once even a set of false teeth. We keep them long enough for the shelves to be full to bursting, and the computerized lists were good enough to locate, in seconds, the missing jacket that the former guest had requested.

Jeri called to ask if I had found the jacket. She said that the former guest was pacing back and forth like a caged tiger, his nerves so on edge that she feared a blowup. That made me curious, so I reassured her that I would bring it to her in five minutes, and I began to search the jacket. The pockets were empty, but when I felt the material, there was a slight bulge. An additional pocket had been sewn under the lining.

I fished around in my top drawer, looking for the small sewing kit I kept there. It was rarely needed except in emergencies because any sewing jobs were handled by one of the chambermaids who worked half time as the hotel seamstress. She could do what I had in mind much better, but there was no time. I snipped a few stitches, just enough to see a wad of bills, and just enough to see that at least one of them was a hundred dollar bill. That much money was probably not clean money, but what the hell. The man was obviously an idiot to have left it behind and not to have remembered for so long. He needed all the help he could get. I would tell Peter as a funny anecdote, and if he would want to follow it through, that would be his business. I resewed the few stitches to look as much like the original as I could, and left in a run. Five minutes was a fair estimate. I rushed down the corridor to the elevators that took my from my cool dark lair deep under the hotel back to the bright sun-filled lobby. I handled him the jacket, without so much as tiny smirk, waited till he had walked through the revolving door, and burst out laughing.

"What?" Jeri asked with a puzzled expression on her face.

I told her and she joined me in laughter.

Now, I thought, I could begin searching the files, so I returned to my office. Becca couldn't stand the tiny over-crowded space and said that it was claustrophobic, but I loved being there. It was almost always quiet and I could work un-disturbed. I know that some of the staff dislike going to our bottom floor, our basement. There are no windows, no day-light, no guests, no breath of outside air, but that place holds the power that runs the hotel. Without the boiler room and the electrical transformer room, nothing would work. The real power behind the staff lies in Patsy's human resources office and in the staff lounge next door, and security is always a locked and secret place, my place. I prefer it to the elegant guest floors. I can see each one of the corridors as a dimly lit tunnel leading to a vague window at the end, punctuated by a row of elevator music pictures in slim gold frames and a rank of doors. Becca says that the gray and rose colors are calming. To me, they are insipid and bland.

The peace and quiet did not even last long enough to open one file. Jeri was back on the phone, apologetic. One of our frequent guests, a business man from Chicago, had returned from a meeting without his credit card, and he was, to say the least, very worried about how he could continue his trip.

This was the kind of discussion best not held in a public lobby. We would meet in his room. I knocked on his door, and a tall thin balding man in his early fifties holding a handkerchief to his nose, opened the door so quickly that I staggered backwards. He was literally wringing his hands in worry. Herbert Timmons had been a guest in the hotel two or three times every month, each time for three nights. We had warned him about the Bartender Convention, but he chose to come anyway. Now he was regretting it.

"Let's sit here, in these armchairs near the window. It's a better way than if I just pace back and forth with you."

He laughed reluctantly and sat down.

"You have a lot of options, and in any case you will have a credit card by the end of the day, or tomorrow noon at the latest."

"How do you know that?" He was a mix of hopeful and truculent.

"I know that, because this is not the first time that I have been able to help in this kind of a situation. It happens and we have a few options, a few things we can do. Plan A is when we figure out exactly where you were and where the card might be."

"I went to a meeting and came back to the hotel. I must have been pick-pocketed. What's plan B?"

"Even so, humor me. I want to start with Plan A. Plan B is a call to the credit card company and a rush order of a new card. Until, the new card comes, the hotel will loan you money. We can't do that for just any guest, but we've known you for so long that you are like part of the family. So try to relax, and we'll give ten minutes to plan A. Okay?"

He muttered a grudging "Okay."

"Remember, anything is possible, so, if you went to a meeting, you paid the cabdriver with cash. We should search the room." He began to shake his head. "Anything is possible. Humor me. You sit and I search.

I began to search methodically. There was no logical place to look, so anything was possible. He could have had the card in his hand, while sitting on the bed, gotten distracted, and put it down. I began to lift the pillows.

"Wait. I know that I had the card with me. I have this damn cold and I didn't want to sneeze and cough throughout my meeting, so I went into the CVS next to the building where I was headed. I used the credit card to buy some cold medicine and some cough drops."

"Is that the last time you saw the card?"

"Yes. No. The meeting was good, and they introduced me to one of their young managers who'll be moving to Chicago. I invited him for coffee at a coffee shop nearby. I took out my card to pay, but he said to put it away. He wanted me to be his guest and said that I could invite him when he got to the Windy City."

"What did you do with the card?"

"Of course, I put it back in my wallet."

"All right, but let's call the coffee shop."

He opened his mouth to reject the possibility.

"No harm to ask. Do you remember which coffee shop it was?"

He shook his head. "But I do remember exactly where it was, because, the area is really part of Chinatown, and he said he'd show me the best coffee place around. I expected something else, but it had great Italian espresso and it was just a block away."

I was pretty sure, I knew, but just in case, I took out my phone and opened google maps. Sure enough, he had gone to Nero's. It was one of the chains we recommended, and I knew the duty manager slightly, so I asked for him, and was rewarded by an answer that made me grin. The card had been left under a napkin, and fortunately had not been swept into the trash. Problem solved all around. In minutes, Timmons, who did not want to delay even a few hours, was in a taxicab on his way back to downtown Boston.

Now I could heave a sigh of relief and get back to the old employee files in my office. I had looked at them often, but never at the files from before my time. They were in three separate categories that were unexpectedly full. I was surprised at how much turnover there had been before Hanley bought the hotel. The first category was of people who had left the hotel on their own, and fortunately, every single file had notations with details and reasons. Some had left because they were new, tried out, and soon realized it wasn't for them. Some had left before the hotel could fire them and some had just up and gone. Then there were quite a few who had been fired for a wide number of reasons, and there were employees who had moved to another hotel in the same chain, either because they had relocated or because they had been promoted. There were many more possible reasons for anger and revenge than I had hoped. Then, I thought again. If Marshall had really been a serial blackmailer, way back then, the chances were good that his victims had, by paying him off, avoided discovery. They would appear to be harmless, and despite what we had thought, they could even still be in the hotel. I reviewed all the reception staff in my mind. It just didn't fit. I would put them aside for the moment, but only if I didn't find a good possibility in the first two categories. I began to make a list on a sheet of lined paper, and the phone rang shrilly, again.

This time it was a really bad one. Jeri's voice was shaky as she told me that the Perkins Family's three year old little girl had disappeared from their room. For a small slice of a second I froze trying to think about the best things to do, and just as quickly I remembered that we had made an emergency plan for just that. There are a few things we really fear. Fires are one of them, and we had already handled a fire this week. Lost children really scare us and in one of my first staff meetings we had talked about what to do, who should do what, and when. We had talked it over time and again until it became almost automatic.

First I sent a text message to the whole staff. "Lock down. Fifth Floor. Three year old child." This sounded dramatic and that was intentional. The doorman would not let anyone leave with any kind of luggage big enough to hold a child, without opening it. Everyone with a master key and the staff that had keys that would fit the rooms on the fifth floor would go there at a run. The person at reception who knew the family best would go to talk to them to get as much information as possible about what had happened

The doorman had the hardest job. He was good at being helpful and nice and now he would have to be tough. We were counting on people accepting the restriction because of the nature of the crisis, but that had never been tested.

Then I called Rebecca, but she didn't answer, so I called Milly in the hope that she was busy in the office.

"Where's Rebecca? She doesn't answer."

"The minute you texted, I tried to reach her. No answer. She went out with Peter. Didn't tell me anything."

"Did she take her master key?"

"No. She always leaves it here."

"Break into her office and grab the key. Come up to the fifth floor."

"On my way."

I took two seconds to text my Mom. Becca disappearing with the investigating detective didn't sound good, but I didn't have any time to think about it.

My plans for action when a child disappeared all sounded so efficient and well planned, but that is not the way it actually happened. When Milly reached me on the fifth floor, I had to send her back down to grill the doorman and find out exactly when he last took a break, and I had forgotten to tell her to do that first.

Anna had brought Marianna who had started late and was still on duty, but when Marianna realized that her job was to open room doors, race in, search the bathroom and the closet for a little girl, she unaccountably became hysterical, and Anna sent her back downstairs. Only much later did we discover that she had been kidnapped by Columbian rebels as a child. If Anna had known, she would have left her behind.

Jeri, who should have gone to talk to the Perkins, sent Russell, who had never met them, because she thought that she was supposed to remain in the lobby. That was actually true, but it assumed that there would be a second receptionist who knew the guests. Russell balked. Actually he didn't really refuse to talk to them. He just convinced me that it would be better if I spoke to them myself. During the few seconds while all this mess was going on, I found myself getting cooler and calmer. Milly, Anna, and Piotr, who had shown up as expected with no fuss, divided the corridor among them and began to rapidly check rooms.

I knew who the Perkins were, but I had never actually met them. Tim and Beth Perkins were spending two weeks in Boston with their two children, and told us that they wanted the hotel even if there was a convention. Their kids could make just as much noise, as any group of barmen, they had written on the email, and Mr. Perkins had often stayed with us on business trips. We had, at their request, put them next to the elevators. That fact was only one of the reasons that I was really worried.

I knocked gently on the door, and it was grabbed open. I would not even have taken note of the room that I had seen hundreds of times if not for the metamorphosis. The family had taken two connecting rooms and this was the obviously the children's room. The drapes were pinned from floor to ceiling with pictures and drawings. On the right side were the scrawls and color splashes of a three year old. On the left were drawings and cut outs of cars and boats and trains and airplanes. One bed had been pushed over to the wall and was partly blocked by the armchair that was wedged next to it, to prevent a small child from falling. By the window, on the floor were scattered puzzles next to two cuddly dolls and a naked Barbie-doll lying on a bed made of numerous miniature outfits. Next to the desk was a different pile with several boxes of Lego pieces, a partially constructed crane and a heap of books. The connecting door was open, and the adjoining room seemed to have been left as is.

I found myself facing a slim attractive woman in her thirties, wearing white capri pants and a black silk boat neck shirt. She had long, straight, black hair, and had no makeup. Her eyes were red, and tear stains marked her face. By the window, stood a slightly stocky tall man, considerably older than his wife, with graying hair and a grim expression. He had thrown his suit jacket on the bed but was still wearing a red necktie on a blue striped shirt. A blond boy, who seemed to be about seven or eight years old, was sitting cross-legged on the carpet looking through the pages of a book. They all looked at me expectantly.

"My name is Betsy Connolly, and I am chief of security in the hotel. First of all, I want to tell you that the hotel staff is already searching, first this floor and then all the other floors. I have to ask you a few questions. What you tell me can help us search better."

"Shouldn't you call the police?" Tim asked brusquely.

"We will if we don't find her in the next five minutes, but we know that she's still in the hotel." I was fudging. We had decided to wait ten minutes, but that depended on the story that they would tell.

"How did you discover that she was missing?"

Tim nodded at his wife and she answered, "My husband was at a meeting, and the kids were napping. Well, Melissa was napping. Bobby usually does fall asleep, so we let him read quietly. I decided to take a shower, and when I finished and came back into the room, she was just gone. Bobby said that he was so absorbed in his book that he never noticed. She would never just walk off. She's not that independent."

"Mom, she always wanders off."

"Bobby, that's enough." Beth answered while her husband maintained silence.

"But, Mom."

Before she could interrupt, I held up my hand in warning. "You know that kids don't always tell their parents everything, and sometimes they see things that we don't. It could be important to hear what he has to say."

Tim moved closer to his wife and gently put his hand on her shoulder. "Let's hear what he has to say." He turned to me. "We were married for a long time before the kids came along. I spend a lot of time, probably too much time, at work, and Beth would like to keep them both small and protected and close to her. I get it. I really do."

We all turned to Bobby, who seemed to be embarrassed.

"My Mom was in the bathroom and Melissa was sound asleep. I know she was sleeping 'cause she makes that fluttering snoring noise when she sleeps. It drives me crazy. I was reading my book, and I never saw her get up, but she can't open the door alone. I know she can't. She tries all the time."

"It is possible that she was finally able to open the door alone, but that would have made noise. Wouldn't you have heard?"

"It's a really good book about Captain Kid. I didn't hear."

"Did you read the whole, whole time?"

Until now, he had remained seated quietly on the floor, but he put his legs straight out in front and stared at them. He twisted and turned, and finally stood up and faced me, literally facing the music.

"Uh.

"Uh." He paused. "Uh." Another pause. "I heard a sort of scratching noise outside the door. I know I'm not supposed to go out alone so I tried to see what was making the noise but

I'm not tall enough to see through the peep hole so I had to open the door, but there was no one there, so I went back to my book."

I didn't even have to question any further. He had not closed the door properly, and absorbed in tales of pirates and treasure, did not notice when his sister awoke, got up, and walked out of the room.

His parents were dumbstruck, but this was no time for recriminations.

"You know that this is a really good thing?"

Already tortured by their imaginations of kidnappers and deviates, they slowly realized what I meant. Both of them sighed in relief. The reality was better, but not a whole lot. A little girl, wandering alone through a hotel, should have been noticed, and should have been reported.

"We will find her. You have to stay here. She could wander back on her own and someone has to be here."

I left the room in relief. The fear and tension there made it hard to breathe, and she had only been missing for an hour or so. If we didn't find her soon, it would get much worse.

Seeing Milly leaving a room, I told her that I would head for my office to search the security cams. They weren't positioned well for small children, but I would try in any case. I told her to wait until they had searched all the rooms on that floor and by then I might have an inkling about where else to search. By then we would have to call the police, too, and it would be an entirely different ball game. I pushed the down button and waited impatiently, bouncing up and down on the balls of my feet. Just as the elevator arrived, I heard a soft whistle. Turning around, I saw Milly holding a small sleeping child in her arms. Long blond curls spilled over her pajama shoulder, and her thumb was in her mouth.

"There was a pile of laundry next to the bed and she was fast asleep on top of it," she whispered.

I knocked gently on the Perkins' door, and Beth opened it. She gasped when she saw Milly and held out her arms. Carefully the still sleeping child was handed over to her mother who was speechless.

"She may have had an adventure and she may have simply sleepwalked. You'll know more when she wakes up. I'd really like to hear what she has to say, but that can wait. We'll be able to talk later."

"Thank you. Thank you. I have no words big enough to express how I feel. I was so afraid. Thank you all."

Milly and I both smiled at her, and watched her close the door.

"One more tragedy averted," the unflappable secretary murmured

I sent a message to the staff telling them that the missing child had been found and that all was well. Then I called Anna and Piotr and asked them to come to the lobby.

"This calls for a drink, at the very least tea or coffee, and I'm buying.

The lobby bar, by the riverside window, had a number of small tables, some with four chairs and most with two. We began with one table and called the waiter to order. Milly had a filter coffee while I prefer getting my caffeine in a diet coke. Both Anna and Piotr ordered black tea. Then I pulled another chair over and enlarged the circle, calling Jeri to join us, leaving Russell to cope alone with the few guests in the lobby. Even before our drinks arrived, we began to tell hotel catastrophe stories with somewhat hysterical laughter. Marianna came up to apologize and Anna, feeling magnanimous, scrunched her chair over to make more room and invited her to join us. The doorman left his post to join us in order to be sure we knew how successfully he had prevented suspects from leaving the hotel, reducing us to helpless laughter.

Guests passed us and looked askance at the group of hotel department managers having an inexplicable party. The mood was festive and relieved and just a bit manic, when we heard a car approach with a screech of brakes. I stood up to look out and saw a red Beemer that looked somehow familiar stop opposite the hotel entrance. A disheveled Rebecca got out and the car sped away. She went through the revolving door and came into the lobby.

If she had known what had preceded our celebration, she would have understood, but I'm pretty sure that she would not have really approved. She believed that you do the right thing, and when you're finished you go on to do the next right thing. But, she didn't know what had preceded our impromptu party, and I winced and prepared for a quiet explosion.

Before anyone could say anything, she marched by us, went over to the door to the reception office, bent down to pick up two of the booties that the police had left behind, slipped them on, and put on rubber gloves from the same pile. Detaching the tape still sealing the room, she walked into the office. We all watched in awe. In minutes she was back out, holding three large ring binders that she presented to Jeri with a flourish. Jeri began to applaud, and was joined by all the rest of us.

I began to explain, but Rebecca said something unclear and laced with anger about not wanting to talk, and disappeared down the corridor, leaving me befuddled.

CHAPTER THIRTEEN

Betsy - Tuesday Evening and Wednesday Morning

It was getting late, and I had, by some miracle gotten Peter to agree to seeing a film with me at the Coolidge Corner Theater. That place had been a fixture of my childhood, but it had changed, along with the times, and become an almost art-film place. The film was, I think, Swedish, and friends of ours had praised it unconditionally. The idea was that he would drive there from work, and I would use the T.

Of course, I got there first, and did a lot of pacing up and down the street until I saw him running through the alley next to the theater that led to the large parking lot that served all of the stores and restaurants in Coolidge Corner. The smells of buttered popcorn that greeted us worked exactly like Proust's madeleine, and for a moment I was nine years old holding on to Rebecca's hand on my way to see a movie.

I quickly realized why Peter had agreed so easily. He was so overworked, so absorbed in his cases, and so ex-hausted that he probably didn't even hear what I had suggested, and once ensconced in the plush comfortable seat, he fell asleep. That was a good thing because the subtitles were distracting and hid parts of the pictures. The story line might have been brilliant in Swedish, but they were murky to me. Just minutes into the film, I found myself in danger of joining Peter. That was silly because we had a perfectly good bed minutes away. I nudged him gently.

"Is it over?"

"It's over for us. Let's go." I smiled and shook my head as he struggled out of sleep.

The cool evening air awakened both of us, and the pizza place across the street was a reminder that we had not yet eaten dinner. Holding hands, we crossed, giggling. The light traffic encouraged jaywalking between the crosswalks, even though one of us was an officer of the law.

We ordered a large pizza, half with mushrooms, for me, and half with pineapple for both of us, and while we were waiting I took a good look at him. His blue eyes were red rimmed and the dark circles underneath made me realize how I messed up. It was as if Marshall's death affected only us. I should have known.

There were so many times that I had seen a case take over his life. Obviously, the circle of family and friends of the victim was left with a burden that would stay with them forever and the maelstrom of emotions at the time could be incapacitating. But life of the cop who handled the case often was changed as well, sometimes forever. This time, I was in the circle and I had forgotten to consider what it was doing to Peter.

Hoping to take his mind off it, I began to tell him about today's adventures and misadventures.

"As if we didn't have enough excitement with murders and drunken guests and bonfires in the middle of our ballroom, we had a lost child today. After that case of the pedophile in the papers last week, we were really stressed out. This was one gorgeous three year old."

I could see that I had his interest.

"You're sitting here with me so I gather that you found her."

"Milly found her sleeping on a pile of laundry in a room opposite her family's room. The father was out of the hotel making more money, the mother had thought that naptime gave her the chance to shower, and the brother has issues. He knows the kid is a wanderer. He's jealous of his new baby sister and he probably left the door open on purpose. Pretty self-defeating if what he wanted was more attention, 'cause for sure she's the one getting it and not him. Poor little guy."

We were interrupted by the waiter bringing us our cokes and a monstrous pizza. We waited until he had gone.

"You sympathize with the criminal?"

"Sure, I had younger siblings, too."

He laughed. "You must have had quite a time. I only had to deal with your firebrand boss and her termagant lawyer." He shook his head like a dog shaking off a bath.

"What?" I asked in shock. "You arrested Rebecca?

"First of all, I didn't arrest anybody. I just brought her in for questioning. I couldn't talk to her at the hotel. There would have been too many interruptions."

"That's bullshit and you know it. What were you thinking? You know she didn't kill anybody."

"I don't know any such thing. Enough pressure and anyone can crack."

"Not Rebecca."

He ignored me. "And second of all, unless I want to take myself off the case I have to investigate wherever the case takes me. You know that."

And I did. I debated with myself about mentioning the blackmail, and decided that it could wait until I had another chance to talk to Rebecca. I didn't want to lie to him or to her, but I wouldn't have to do it if I just skipped lightly over telling when I had found out about the email that Rebecca had received after the fact.

"I have to talk with her."

"It's late. All of us have had a bad day, including your boss. It would probably be much better to wait until tomorrow. I would go with you, but I doubt that I'll be her favorite person for a while."

"Pete, I have totally lost my appetite for this pizza. If you're still hungry, I'll wait, but if not, let's just go."

"It'll probably taste better cold tomorrow morning. We'll take a doggy bag."

I couldn't help laughing. Peter had introduced me to the pleasures of leftover pizza, known only to true pizza lovers. Pizza could be handled cold, and so could Rebecca. I would head in to the hotel early the next morning, before the morning shift. I was ready to bet that she would be there.

We both fell into bed exhausted. Peter slept like a log, not moving at all, and I tossed and turned. When I finally fell asleep, I dreamt of jail cells and a furious Rebecca who shouted at me for going to the movies without her. Then she shouted at me for crossing the street alone, and suddenly I was nine years old, and just as suddenly, I was awake.

I dressed quietly, leaving Peter still dead to the world, and left the apartment. Reaching the hotel, I checked to see if Rebecca's car was there and went to look for her. The office was empty, and reception told me that she had slept in the hotel. They gave me her room number, with a warning that she had asked for a late wakeup call, a warning that I unfortunately ignored.

I knocked on the door and she pulled it open, looking as if she had not slept a minute.

"Are you all right? They told me you were here, that you slept here. What's wrong?"

"What's wrong is that I just went to sleep after a night working to find our murderer. What's even more wrong is that before that I spent hours being grilled by your boyfriend who suspects me of murder because you couldn't keep your mouth closed. I'm going back to sleep, and the last person I want to see right now is you. If you want to skip the morning briefing feel free."

I fled and heard the door slam hard behind me. When I turned the corner, I pulled out my cell phone. My only thought was to get to Peter, but even in the midst of my almost hysteria, I knew that it would be a foolish move. If I took the T, it would take hours and he might not even be at the station. If I took the car, there would be no parking, I would get a ticket, and, again, he might not even be there.

He answered on the first ring and an avalanche of sound fragments poured out.

"Betsy, sweetheart, slow down. I can't understand a word you're saying. What's wrong?"

With a forced calm, I answered. "Rebecca said that it's my fault that she was arrested. She said that I told you something that made you arrest her."

"I didn't arrest her. Why should she say that?"

"She didn't exactly say that, but she did say it was all my fault. What did you tell her?"

"I never mentioned your name, and you never told me anything about anything. Look, I'm tied up now, but in an hour or so I'll be free and I'll come over. We'll talk with her and straighten this out."

"She doesn't want to talk to me," I said sadly.

"She'll talk to me. Can you wait an hour? I promise, I'll be there as soon as I can."

I nodded and mumbled "Okay," and closed the phone.

I didn't want to deal with anybody, guest or staff, and I couldn't imagine eating breakfast so I headed for my retreat. On the way, I saw that the lights were on in the human resource office. It was hard to believe that Patsy's minimal replacement had actually come in early, but the door was locked and the office was empty. I shrugged and continued to my office, where I spent the next two hours doing nothing.

When the phone rang, I jumped. It was Peter and he was waiting to join me in Rebecca's office. I rushed upstairs, grabbed his hand and headed for the administration area. Milly was not at her desk, so I tapped on the door and walked in as if everything was normal with Peter close behind.

Shockingly, the room was full.

Rebecca looked at us and, addressing Peter, said sternly, "This is a private staff meeting. Could you please wait in the lobby?"

He was holding my hand, and when he turned around and left, I went with him.

"That was a rout, huh?"

I didn't answer. We sat by the window and ordered coffee that I didn't really want. My stomach was roiling and I breathed in and out slowly to control the sudden nausea. All this while, Peter was patting my hand. We sat there, not talking, not really seeing the view, just waiting. A few minutes later I saw Jeri heading for reception, and behind her, Piotr. They both smiled at us tentatively. We stood together and walked back to the office. Wordlessly, Milly opened Rebecca's door and motioned us to enter.

Before she could say a word, Peter had marched up to her and begun to speak.

"I have been trying to figure out why you think that Betsy told me anything. She didn't. She didn't have to. I have Marshall's computer."

We both gasped. That was dumb. Of course he had the computer. He would know everything on it that wasn't password protected and with Jake's computer hacking skills he would know all the rest, too.

"How did you think I knew about the blackmail? Betsy didn't say a word to me." He looked in my direction. "We will have a little talk about that, too, my love."

A gurgle was my only response.

"I'm figuring that for some reason, you never saw the email. He asked for a read return and there was none. If you had seen an email from your reception manager, you would have automatically answered the read return because that's what you do, and that would have been before you saw the contents. Am I right? That is what you do?"

I nodded.

"Let me just think a bit about it out loud. You were truly and convincingly incensed by the accusation, and you are not that good an actor."

Keeping no expression on my face, I thought, 'She is, she is.'

"After you came back from the station, I bet you searched your mail and found the threat. That is the timing that I think is correct, and if it is true, you had no reason to kill him because you didn't know. Unless there was some other reason, but let's leave that aside for now."

He winked at me and continued. I stole a quick glance at Rebecca and she appeared to be mesmerized.

"Another possibility is that you are that good an actor and you had seen the blackmail threat, but I still believe that it was after he was dead, partly because of that unanswered read return, and mostly because I know you. If he had been alive, you would have marched into his office and yelled at him. You might have fired him, but you wouldn't have killed him. How am I doing, so far?"

He looked at her and then at me but we both kept silent.

"I'm guessing something else. He threatened to tell if you don't pay, and you didn't pay, because you didn't know, so he probably told someone. The person he told would have been Hanley, but Hanley's out of the country. Did he get to him before he left? It could very well be, and if he did, and if Hanley told you, which would have been just what he would do, you would have had another excellent reason not to have killed Marshall. There would have been no reason, because it was just too late, and the reason you didn't tell me is because, being a basically honest person, you just don't figure things that way. Neither did Betsy, for the same reason. I, on the other hand, deal with so much dishonesty that my mind works that way. Am I right?"

He looked at Rebecca triumphantly, and she, having risen from her seat during his monologue, just stood there with her mouth open. Finally she nodded.

"You are awfully smart."

"You are, too, Madame hotel manager, but not in the dark world that Marshall inhabited. Remember that this is what I do. Now can we please start over?"

I had been listening, quietly, a change for me, to Peter doing his stuff. I had wanted to tell him from the beginning, and how right I was. Now, I pitched in. "Rebecca, this morning you said something about spending the night finding the killer. Isn't this the right time to ask for help?"

She laughed wryly. "I spent most of the night looking at old hotel program data. I couldn't use Marshall's computer, because you have it, but I could get into his files through

Patsy's computer. I found someone that he apparent caught cheating, and I'm betting he blackmailed him, but I couldn't find his name in the employment files although he did work here. Maybe Marshall somehow erased him."

"I should have known that was what you were doing. You left the light on when you left Patsy's office

"It was pretty late and I was already half asleep."

"What was the name?" I was curious because when I had searched the employee data base I had pretty much memorized all the names, without even trying.

"I don't know his name but his username was ANDYP."

"There are a few possibilities. Peter, if we go back to my office, I can find it."

"Then let's go."

The three of us marched out and turned to the staff elevator. We rode down in silence and hurried to my office where there was barely enough room for us.

Riffling through the files, in minutes I came up with a probable name.

"How does Anderson Porter sound?"

"It doesn't sound like any of the names I saw of staff who were fired or quit,"

I knew something she didn't but I took pity on her and so I was not going to drag it out. "That's because he's still on the open files."

"But there is no one here with that name."

"Because he didn't quit or get fired. He was transferred to New York, probably because he asked to be transferred and was accepted at the Manhattan Hanley. Staff who are transferred are still in the file. What's more they keep the same employee ID card and the system doesn't eliminate them."

In a strangled voice she said, "I know that. I kept my card."

Peter interrupted. "What did you find out about him? What did he do?"

"If he had a cash paying guest for one night only, he took the money and gave the guy a room without putting him in the computer. Then he marked the room as dirty so housekeeping would clean the room. It's not as uncommon as it should be, but it does happen. He, however, was turning it into an industry and it wasn't hard for Marshall to catch him."

"So Marshall did catch him?"

"Yes he did, but instead of reporting it, he protected him."

"Voila, blackmail. If Marshall got greedy, maybe our ANDYP got fed up."

I looked at her. If she had only gone to Peter in the beginning, we would have already known. Maybe we would have even already caught him, but if it had been Porter, he was doubtlessly back in New York laughing at us. Peter had not wasted any time in recriminations, and was already on the phone.

"Hi, Jake. I need information on a first name Anderson last name Porter, probable residence somewhere in New York City, employed at the Manhattan Hanley Hotel."

He listened for a minute and then continued. "Yeah, yeah. I know. If he's in New York, it'll be a bitch to get him back here, so please get started as soon as you can. I also want to know if you can find evidence that he was in Boston a few days ago." He hung up and turned to us.

"Jake's a magician, but even magic takes time. Has anyone here had a chance to have breakfast?"

We both shook our heads and Peter continued.

"That sounds like a good idea of how to pass the time while we wait."

Walking into the dining room, I saw that there were still a large number of convention guests eating a late breakfast. We took a table as far away from them as possible and began to eat.

Rebecca had received a reprieve. She had really feared an accusation of murder, and Peter had just been kind enough to explain why she was no longer even a minor suspect. She ate enough for all the hours that she was unable to eat. I watched in amazement because she was always so careful not to overdo. She got three eggs sunny side up with slices of bacon from the breakfast cook working at the buffet and sopped them up with crusty rye bread. The she took a plate of slices of various kinds of hard cheese and ate them with toast points. She took jam and butter and ate them with the remainders of the toast. She did all this while drinking cup after cup of coffee.

"Wow, lady, you must have been some kind of hungry." Peter commented. She looked up at him, down at her plate, and blushed. I laughed. It felt right. Now all we had to do was catch the killer.

Then Peter's phone rang. He answered it, listened and turned to us bemused.

"Jake has just gotten started, and first he did financials. Credit cards. Stuff like that. Anderson Porter is in Boston."

CHAPTER FOURTEEN

Rebecca - Wednesday Morning

The wakeup call left me just enough time either to shower or to eat breakfast, and I decided to get clean and maybe even awake. Food could wait. When I walked into my office, all of them, except for Betsy, were waiting.

As usual, Milly had added all the chairs in her office to mine, making the space crowded and uncomfortable. There was one empty chair for Betsy and Patsy's assistant had long ago been told that she need not bother to come. That was after she had monopolized the meeting with irrelevancies.

The chef was quiet, not having really been a participant in yesterday's excitement and all the others were bubbling over with excitement. At first I thought they were talking about me, and it seemed way out of proportion, but they could barely wait to share yesterday's triumph over the lost child. At first, I had no idea what they were talking about but once I grasped the story, I could only share the enjoyment. Any other outcome would have been a tragic nightmare. I heaped praise on them, but they were quick to credit Betsy. I may have been extremely pissed off at her, but they were right. She was super good at her job and I was very lucky to have her. Now, if I could only figure out how to make the personal part work, too. I kept on trying and getting it wrong.

Finally, after a lot of laughter and jokes, we got the meeting back on track, and were going over arrivals and departures, when, preceded by an almost non-existent tap on the door, Betsy walked in, followed by Peter. I should have nodded hello and asked someone to bring in an extra chair, but, I am ashamed to say, I threw them out. The others looked at me strangely, but said nothing. We finished in record time and when everyone else had left, they came back.

I was determined not to say a word and I clenched my jaws. I wanted to hear how Betsy could excuse what she had done to me. I was tired and angry and ready for a fight. Then, almost nonchalantly, Peter punctured the balloon.

"I have been trying to figure out why you think that Betsy told me anything. She didn't. She didn't have to. I have Marshall's computer."

We both gasped, and I realized that Betsy was as surprised as I was. I should have realized, and few words could explain how stupid I felt. What was worse and even more embarrassing was that Peter had more or less figured out exactly what had happened. If only he had told me what and how and why he knew, yesterday would have been entirely different. He was playing the objective fair-minded, even handed cop. Phooey to that, but I was in no condition to criticize.

I had been holding a lot inside and it felt good to let it all go free, to let it gush out. I told them about my discoveries, feeling pretty good about having figured out how to get the computer to give up what it knew, but it didn't really interest them. I wanted to show them how smart I'd been but they only wanted the last line. Who? I didn't know who. I just had his computer username. I thought that was a lot. We could get through to the chain IP manager and he would be able to search his files and get us the name, but Betsy, being Betsy, knew how to turn the username into his identity without outside help.

We rode the elevator down to the basement floor where I had spent most of the night, and went into her office to search the files. She unlocked the filing cabinet that held all the employee files and hovered over it. Peter sat at her desk leaning backward on the desk chair precariously with his back to the wall of cubby holes that held all the lost and found from the last months. I sat on the visitor's chair and chewed on my fingernails.

After only minutes, I heard Betsy murmur a subdued "Yes." And saw her grin. I hadn't been able to find him, because I had totally forgotten that employees who moved to a different Hanley hotel stayed in the same file. In afterthought, it was obvious. Why should he leave? He had a good deal going. New York was the capitol of walk-ins, the guests who just walked in off the street. ANDYP was probably raking it in, and the only person who could spoil it was now conveniently dead.

I could find him easily through the chain, unless he had decided to move his operations to a different Manhattan hotel, but Peter wanted to do it through his sources, so that there would be no chance for him to find out that we were on to him. He called the station to talk to Jake, the computer expert. I had gotten to know him well, and not only was he a master at using police computer resources, he was the best hacker that I knew.

While he worked his magic, we decided to eat breakfast. Betsy had been too anxious to eat, Peter had been too busy, and I had been too sound asleep. Reaching the dining room, I realized that I was ravenous. I was giddy with relief at first but as I ate, I relaxed more and more. If I had been alone, I would have cried. The police would get Marshall's killer even if they had to extradite from New York, and I was finally, thoroughly, totally off the hook. What is more, if the motive was ANDYP's attempt to get rid of a blackmailer, and he had taken off, no one else was in danger. Suddenly I became aware of the clink of silverware and glasses and of the soft music that played in the background. I felt as if I had been locked inside an impervious bubble and that now I was free.

Then Jake called and spilled cold water on all of us. ANDYP was in Boston. He had just used his credit card in a coffee shop on Washington Street near Downtown Crossing.

"Why?" Betsy asked, echoing my thoughts. "Why would he still be here?"

"Well, he might have unfinished business, like a few more hoteliers to knock off."

We laughed nervously.

"Or, he might get off on the risk taking, or he might want to know what the police are doing, or he just might want to tour historic Boston. If he's here, I want to know what he looks like. I'll call Jake back to get us his DMV photo,"

"I can do better than that. We have his staff card picture on file, but I'll have to go back down to my office. You guys stay here and finish your coffee. I'll be right back."

Most of what Betsy has on her computer, she can get on mine, too, but I figured she was hoping that we would get back on some kind of a normal footing if we could talk alone.

"You know that I had no choice. I shouldn't have been on this case, but we're short handed now and the chief wanted me to handle it as long as everything was by the book."

"I'm glad you realized that I had no real logical reason to kill him, although I was pretty mad, but we both know that when people are angry enough, they do illogical things. The truth is that I really did go home and I didn't get back until almost seven."

"I know. You messed with your lawn watering controls, and got sprayed by an errant sprinkler and cursed and went into your house to dry off. You drank a cup of coffee and munched on toast standing by the kitchen window. You washed the cup and saucer, and walked out of the kitchen. You turned on the radio, rather loudly, and about an hour later turned it off and left the house,"

I gaped at him.

"You have a very nosy neighbor. By the book, remember."

"So you know I didn't do it. It wasn't just the logic."

"By the book, Ma'am, by the book."

The image of Marloo suddenly appeared in my head. She had told me that he would do it by the book not despite our friendship, but because of our friendship. Suddenly, I remembered. Marloo would be expecting me.

"Peter, tell me the truth. Do I still need a lawyer?"

"It hurts like hell to admit it, because you are talking about that fireball on wheels, but I think you should still keep her in the picture until this is all over. Even though you're covered for the time of the murder, you had an excellent reason to want him dead."

I called her while we were still talking.

"Marloo, something has come up and I have to postpone our meeting."

"Darling, there cannot be anything more important than your life. You shouldn't delay our meeting."

"Yes, I really understand, and it's only a short postponement. I know how important it is. Even Peter thinks so."

"I bet he does." There was a long silence. "So you have been talking to Peter? That is a really bad idea. I cannot approve."

"Marloo, I have no choice about it. After all I still have to manage the hotel and the police are investigating a murder here, but I understand what you say and I promise to be very circumspect."

She humphed loudly and both said goodbye.

"You didn't exactly put her in the picture." Peter said with a grin.

"No," I mused thoughtfully. "I will as soon as we see how this new information pans out."

Betsy walked into the dining room and looked at us. She saw that we were talking and laughing, and approached, holding several sheets of paper.

"I printed a few. I also sent them to your mail if you need more."

We each took a sheet and studied. An undistinguished average-looking Anderson Porter looked back. His brown hair was cut almost short enough to be a Marine boot camp haircut. His brown eyes looked serious and friendly, his cheeks were a tiny bit full, he had a slightly pug nose and he was smiling, showing white even teeth. Alongside were descriptions. He was five feet ten and weighed a hundred and eighty four pounds. Disgustingly normal, even though he was apparently heavier than he looked in the head shot. Still, he would blend into any background.

I turned to Peter. "Should we be worried that he's still here? Will you be able to find him?"

"Oh, we'll find him. He used his credit card once and he'll use it again and we'll be on top of him. Worst case, if we don't get him here, the New York City cops will get him for us."

"We should be able to find him on the security cams the night of the murder," Betsy mused. You can get the pictures in your office."

We rose from the table, thanked the waiter, and trooped back to my office where Betsy took over my chair to find the security cam program on the computer. I was happy to let her do it, because I already had experience with how hard it was to operate.

"Here we are on Monday morning at the hotel entrance. How far back should we go?"

I answered her. "Not many people at that hour. You can speed back to find people going in and out and slow down only when you see someone."

We saw me arriving, and the taxi and the angry guest departing. We saw another guest, dressed in a long raincoat, with a small suitcase leave without a backward glance. It wasn't clear if it was a man or a woman. Then, going back in time, for a long, long time there was nothing. There was a female guest arriving with a carry-on, probably after a late flight, and then more nothing. When we passed the photos taken before midnight and were looking at Sunday night, Betsy looked at us questioningly.

"Keep on a few more hours back. Do you know who was on the evening shift?"

"Yeah," she answered. "As a matter of fact, I do. It was Marshall."

At about seven, we saw an arrival with a suitcase. It was Porter wearing a voluminous raincoat that hid his body, but he looked up at the camera and smiled. This was a camera that also was projected into reception, and if Marshall was looking, he would see him before he walked in the door. The image I got was not at all hostile. If this is the way things started, then it would have been easy for Porter to get close enough to shoot Marshall at close range. But there was a suitcase. Had he slept in a room at the hotel before doing the deed? I had heard something yesterday from someone that had to do with to that question. The trouble was that I couldn't remember exactly where I had heard it and what it was. I tried, too hard, to recollect, but, whatever it was, the memory remained elusive.

Betsy had been sitting on my chair, but she jumped up excitedly. "I just thought of something. He can get in and out another way, too, with his staff card through the timekeeper. It'll be a lot easier to find his name on the list."

"What's a timekeeper? Isn't a timekeeper a watch?"

Betsy and I chuckled, and she looked at me. She wanted me to give him the answer. I understood her reluctance.

"A timekeeper used to be where a security officer sat and checked in the workers as they entered, but today it's just like other places have, an employee's entrance with a time clock. You probably have one, too."

He nodded, but I wasn't finished, because it could be important that he understood.

"Within the year we're replacing it with a thumbprint reader."

He raised an eyebrow and asked, "Is that to make it faster and easier for the staff?"

"Not really. You see, a hotel has a multitude of ways for the staff to steal, and we want to prevent it. No, I'm not explaining this right. Most of the people who work here earn minimum wage. They are mostly pretty poor, and they are exposed daily to rich people and a wealthy way of life. It's smart to eliminate temptations as much as we can. It's not just that we don't want to be robbed, even of work hours, but we don't want them to become thieves. It begins when they walk in, and there have been cases where one person entered someone else's card as a favor, so that the other person could come late. Having a real timekeeper would eliminate that, and the bigger hotels do just that. For the smaller hotels, the cost of the extra person is more than the cost of a thumb print reader. I hope that it's clear. It's like the Jewish Talmud says, 'honor the other, but not with excessive trust'. The only problem is that no matter how many safeguards you put in, there will always be a way to get around them if someone like Porter learns how to manipulate the system."

Betsy turned to Peter to explain the technicality. "The time clock is basically a computer. It registers the names, and the departments, and the shifts that are already programmed in by each department head. Someone from another hotel, without a department would stand out."

"So why didn't anyone notice the strange name," Peter asked.

I answered him. "Even I can answer that. We don't even print out the list unless we have to check up on someone. Nobody would see that there's a strange name unless you looked, but if you do look, it's easy to find."

Betsy looked at us with a wry smile. "The human yoyo will go back down again. That list is only on Patsy's computer. She's the only one who might need it, so we don't bother to get it anywhere else." She walked out, leaving the office door open. Peter got up and closed it gently.

"Sometimes my beloved fiancée forgets that not every conversation is meant for anyone who happens to pass by."

"Fiancée? Well, well, well. Congratulations. "

"Oops. I wasn't supposed to say anything until she feels it's the right time to tell her mother. She said that if she says anything too early, the church will be booked, the priest alerted, and the wedding cake baked. I admit to being very happy, and I have to keep remembering not to share it."

I laughed. "She is absolutely right, and I cannot remember a word you said." I winked at him.

I looked at the pile of letters that Milly had put in my inbox. I wouldn't be able to do anything with them this morning, and although we were waiting, I would restrain myself from doing something so impolite, especially after making peace with Peter, but he saw me looking.

"Go ahead. I don't mind, and I don't know what's keeping Betsy."

"I'll only do the short ones."

I skimmed all the letters, putting most aside for fuller attention, and marking the rest with notes telling Milly what to do. Finally, Betsy, somewhat out of breath, came back.

"Sorry, Anna stopped me. One of the girls lost her necklace, and she wanted me to help her look."

"Did you find it?" I knew that even cheap costume stuff had enormous importance to these girls, and some of them had jewelry that had been brought from their homeland and that had great nostalgic value.

"Sure. With both Anna and me using our eyes, we found it on the floor of her office."

Suddenly, it all came together and I remembered. Without explaining to Betsy or Peter, I immediately dialed Anna's number.

"Anna, Hi. It's Rebecca. Remember those rooms that kept on showing up as dirty when they should have been clean? Were they different rooms every time, or the same one."

"How did you guess? It was the same one each time, room 232, but today it won't happen. The room is booked. Either that or someone's gonna get a really bad surprise."

Curious, I asked, "Who is the arrival?"

"Just a minute. I'm checking. It was a booking that Marshall, rest his soul, made with instructions not to change the room. It's a staff booking but I can't make out what Marshall wrote about which of our hotels. It's an A. Porter."

"Thanks, Anna," I spoke in a strangled voice. When we had gone over the arrivals and departures, I had not really been listening. I winced, and silently berated myself. We include the lists of arrival in the morning briefing just because some of us might recognize a name.

Betsy was looking at me with a smile. She had immediately understood why I had asked, and when I hung up, she gave me a high five. Peter looked back and forth at us, completely in a fog.

"Help me out here. Why are you both looking so smug? What just happened?"

"I never really had a chance to explain what Porter did and why Marshall could blackmail him. He was stealing rooms."

Peter looked even more confused. "You can't steal a room."

"In a hotel, you can. He was giving rooms to guests who stayed for only one night and paid cash, without registering them. He put the money in his pocket and when it was late enough in the evening, he marked the room dirty so that it would get cleaned in the morning. That, Mr. Policeman, is stealing. He was doing it a lot and making enough money to make it worthwhile to pay blackmail until something went wrong. Well, what he did for guests, he did for himself here. He knew his way around, and somehow, he found a way to get to a computer. Once he had a hotel computer, he could log on and do whatever he wanted."

Betsy added with glee, "We have him now. We know exactly where he's going to be tonight."

"Hold on a minute, love. There is no we. You two are staying out of it. This is a dangerous man and when it's late enough to be sure that he is here, I'll bring backup. We'll wait till he comes in, and catch him. You two stay away from whatever room it is. And what room is it?"

Regretfully, I answered with the room number. I had no wish to tangle alone with a killer, but after the awful experience of being a potential accused murderer, I did want to be around when the real killer was caught. I looked at Betsy, and she winked. Peter left to organize things from the station, leaving us alone.

"He can't stop us from hanging around the second floor, can he?" I asked Betsy.

She wrinkled her brow in thought. "Yes, he can. He'll block off the entire floor, but I have a sort of an idea. I'll need some time to figure out exactly how we can work it. Anyway, we have most of the day. I don't know about you, but I do have some actual work that I have to do. How about we meet at lunchtime?"

I nodded and, shaking my head in wonder, watched her half walk half run out of the office. Betsy seemed to take every single thing in her stride. I was filled with admiration. We had enjoyed some good times in the past and I wondered why that hadn't been true lately.

Milly stuck her head through the open door. "Now that you're free," she murmured. "There are a few checks to sign. It is that time of the month, you know."

She had to know how much I disliked signing checks, because every time check signing time came around, my cursing was loud enough for her to hear. It used to be much worse when almost every invoice didn't match the requisition, and mistakes in arithmetic were common, but that was only when we all began at the hotel and Hanley was an unknown quality. The buyer and the stores-man and the accounting department soon learned that I actually checked, and after redoing a large number of checks, the process improved. The suppliers also learned that if we ordered a hundred pounds of something, we paid for a hundred pounds. That took longer and didn't make me many friends, but it worked, and costs went down. I still checked and hated the busy work. 'Bean counters actually love doing this,' I muttered.

"I heard that." Milly said with a mock stern expression.

"Okay. Okay. Ready for whatever you throw at me."

She walked back to her desk, picked up an impossibly high pile of papers and placed them carefully on my desk. I groaned.

I groaned, not just because there was such a large quantity, but because it should have been a computer file sent to my computer, a file that included all the documents, compared them, and notified me of any discrepancies. I wasn't getting a computer file, because the inventory program was a hungry beast that had to be fed every bit of data. When too many people were out sick, the computer did not get fed enough, and this was the result.

Almost as annoying as the need to check someone else's math was the need to rearrange someone else's mess. What had started out in the accounting office as a neat pile of flimsy pink or white requisition forms attached to flimsy computer copies of the order forms attached to a variety of invoices attached to pale green checks did not remain neat for long. The staples tore the flimsy paper and by the time the pile arrived on my desk, the forms were often not attached to the right papers. Before I could compare numbers, I had to match things up. This was more aggravation than I felt like handling especially today, but there was little choice, so I started to shuffle the papers like floppy playing cards. In no time, my desk was covered with pastel colors.

Milly came in to check on my progress and the draft made by the door scattered a mess or errant pink, blue, white, green, and yellow onto the floor.

She took one look at me and murmured, "Sorry, sorry. Nothing urgent. Sorry."

She backed out, closing the door slowly and carefully behind her.

The whole process took hours. Worst were the food and beverage invoices because each one was connected to a whole mess of different purchase orders covering a long period of time. We didn't order milk once, we ordered it every day and the quantity would depend on the occupancy, and so on. By the time that I finished signing every check that would be cosigned by Hanley, or in this case by his CFO, I was not in a very good mood. My earlier elation had totally evaporated.

Milly, who timorously had come in to take away the pile of documents, took one look at me and suggested the usual remedy. "Since all this mess with Marshall began, you haven't had a chance to walk. It's quiet now, why don't you take an hour off? I know that you're waiting for something to happen. You're going to start pacing back and forth soon and you're going to drive me nuts."

I began to shake my head and explain that I had too much to do, but I stopped. There wasn't anything that could not wait. Doing the invoices and checks had been irritating, but it had been an automatic kind of work. It would be hard to concentrate on anything more complicated and I had time before the police would return to set the trap for Porter. My running shoes and a stack of clean socks were placed neatly on the bottom shelf of the bookcase behind the desk. I bent down to remove my medium heels and knee highs and put on a pair of socks and the shoes. I had no intention of running, just fast walking, and I didn't have to change my clothes. I walked purposefully out of the office, down the stairs from the mezzanine floor and through the lobby. If anyone, seeing me, would have wanted to approach, the look on my face and my quick passage would put them off.

I walked out of the hotel through an almost palpable wall of indifferent air. I loved being in the hotel and I spent more time there than anywhere else. It was challenging and exciting. It was a place where I daily created a new entity, a new performance, where everyone, guests and staff, depended on me. It was my playing field, but it was never tranquil and it was always aimed at me. Outside the hotel there was another world where I could move in any way I wanted, without making a real difference

Outside, there was a roar of traffic on the nearby highway, with nearby brakes squealing and horns honking. There were gasoline dirty smells of the city mixed with the aroma of freshly cut grass and seasonal flowers into a heady perfume. I closed my eyes, breathed in, and felt tension wash away. The trees near the hotel formed a leafy lacy canopy over my head and shaded me from the early summer sun. It was indeed a different universe.

My work is always so 'now' combined with a portentous 'tomorrow'. What happens in the world currency markets today will affect our occupancy and our income tomorrow. The revolution breaking out in some corner of the world today will affect my sales. The race riot somewhere else will actually help us and the race riot here will kill us. Today's announcement of a new app will change the way we handle reservation. It's exciting and inspiring, but it does nothing to evoke tranquility. That is probably the reason that I love to study history. History is mostly yesterday. It's tomorrow, too, but much much slower. History is exciting and inspiring, and it can also be tranquil.

So every time I went out I would walk down the center of Commonwealth Avenue along the mall and I would visit history. First, I would visit my favorite statue which was put in place only a few years ago, the 'Women's Memorial'. There I could find Lucy Stone and the slave turned poetess, Phillis Wheatley, and good old Abigail Adams. Unlike the statesmen and soldiers further down the Commonwealth Mall, these women have no need of pedestals and are right down at ground level.

The day had been so fraught with tension that I almost ran to the green grass and flower bordered walkway, but the vibrant tapestry of everyday life in the Back Bay grabbed my attention. We were so close to the ever encroaching Boston University that many students had found tiny apartments in the area. Some young people sat on the steps leading to the street from apartments that had been illegally subdivided to cash in on the flood of college students. Dressed in a riot of colors and a combination of winter and summer clothes, they lifted young faces to drink in the early summer sun. Tiny white wires led to their ears as if evolution had provided them with useful appendages that we, the real adults, did not have, and some of them swayed to music only they could hear.

A pair of teenage girls, out from school early, or skipping class, hung, almost entwined, on a stoop railing, as they texted and giggled over responses on each others' smartphones. Like many of their age, adamantly determined to break away from convention, they were actually in uniform. Long straight hair, one of honey and one of blue-black, streamed down their backs and cropped tops showed more skin than their school would have allowed had they been in class. Their skinny jeans not only demonstrated that the honey blond should never wear anything so tight without a serious diet, but when they swung around and sat on the steps, I saw that their jeans had gaping holes on the knees, and probably cost a great deal more for it. I looked at the blond with sympathy because I could wear A-line skirts and pants with tailored pleats to hide my dietary transgressions.

Some of the university lecturers who also lived in the area were familiar because they would come in occasionally to have coffee at our coffee shop in the lobby. I smiled and nodded a silent hello to the couple walking with their toddler between them, connecting them with his tiny chubby baby hands. The professor, whose name I never knew, wore gray jogging pants and a gray sweatshirt, offset by the navy blue Sikh turban over his bearded cinnamon face. His wife, who was not a Sikh and who taught anthropology, was a walking rainbow with flaming orange swirling loose pants topped by a long tunic of canary yellow and a long blue-green gauze scarf. She smiled happily as she and her husband swung the tiny little boy between them, and, seeing me, smiled again, crinkling black eyes in her lovely coffee cream face.

I immediately began to feel better. The dull feeling of fear that had followed me since Sunday night began to ebb. Outside the hotel, the world, with its mass of varied individual concerns, continued to exist. My problems, bad as they were, got smaller in proportion. I had begun to think that all my success, all the control I showed, all my always knowing what to do, were all a big bluff, and that under it all was a fake, me. That somehow I had succeeded in fooling myself and all around me. Much as it hurt, I realized that there was a lot I didn't know about what really went on the hotel. Wise Bridget had provided the key for me to use. Despite what she thought, I talked a lot with my staff members, but she had guessed correctly that it was always business, never personal. If I really wanted to know about all the currents under the surface, that would have to change. I could do it. My optimism began to return. All I had needed was to step out of the bubble hotel, and see the real world. I jauntily continued walking towards Comm Ave with the smile lingering on my face.

When I reached the first statue, I paused and then, as usual, circled the statues. When I again faced back in the direction from which I had come, something in my visual frame shifted. Momentarily, someone walking behind me had also paused. Despite the midday heat, I shivered.

It was impossible to see whose steps had stopped when I had stopped, but I was suddenly absolutely positive that someone was following me. None of the joggers and strollers looked even remotely like Anderson Porter. There were two men jogging more or less together. One was black and one was extremely thin with long floppy blond hair. They were pretty far back and both wore Harvard crimson. They were obviously too young as well.

The woman wearing lime green running shorts and a skimpy halter of the same electric color with a messy topknot of blond curls that threatened to topple was walking, not running despite her jogger's outfit. She looked slightly familiar and I thought that I had seen her several times when I had walked this route. I assumed that she lived somewhere in the Back Bay.

The old countess was also familiar. She probably was no countess, but that was the name I had given her for her haughty elegance. Today she wore pearl gray to match the miniature poodle that pranced beside her on a silver leather leash. Perfectly coiffed white hair, a silky pearl gray blouse of long sleeves and matching tailored slacks completed the outfit that ignored the warm early summer weather. She certainly had not stopped. She never stopped for anyone, except to scoop the dog's tiny crap into a plastic bag whenever it became necessary. A tall monk with a dark leathered sculptured face wearing a brown cassock strolled behind me, lost in fascination with the statues and the buildings on both sides of the mall. He paid no attention to the people who shared the walk, and to the stares that accompanied him. He was too old, too dark, and too gaunt to be Porter.

A possibility was the young couple pushing a baby carriage together. She appeared to be in her late teens and had stringy mousy hair, pale cheeks, no makeup, and a look of bliss on her face. She was wearing a flowered house dress and looked as if she had just fallen out of bed. He was slightly overweight and bald and his belly strained at the buttons of the red and blue checked shirt that he wore untucked. If that was Porter, he was a great actor. The two of them were looking into each other's eyes and they were hanging all over each other and kissing. Any progress forward was coincidental and they seemed oblivious to their surroundings.

Never the less, I had no doubt that I was being followed and had no idea why. Maybe the police still had their doubts and were tailing me, and maybe Porter was looking for another chance to get rid of a hotel manager. I told myself that it was nonsense and that I was not going to let anyone spoil my walk. I set out again, but just before I reached the statue of Samuel Eliot Morison, perched on his boulder, I had a strange feeling at the back of my neck. Either I was straining a muscle by constantly looking over my shoulder or this was my subconscious warning me that I was being followed. I quickly walked to the other side of the rear admiral and peaked around him back towards the back. The serious joggers had long passed me. The countess was still gamely marching on. The couple that had made me want to shout 'get a room' had fallen far behind, the monk had disappeared, and the blond not quite jogger was still there struggling on.

Again I told myself that I was being silly and that I was imagining my stalker. I tried to enjoy the walk, but that was like trying to tell myself not to think about dieting. All I would think about would be dieting. Now, all I could think about was being stalked and trying to figure out why, and what he could do to me when I was in such a public place. My walk was ruined and I figured that I might as well go back to the hotel as quickly as possible. I walked on through the mall.

What the hell did I care? Let them follow me. What could anyone do to me surrounded by traffic on both sides and multitudes of Bostonians out for a walk? I carried on, not stopping at the remaining statues as I usually did, until I reached the Boston Gardens. They are beautiful and green and cool and unexpected with lakes and the famous Boston swan-boats, but there are too many isolated spots along the way, and I was taking no chances. During the brisk walk, my mood had swung back and forth from concern, even fear, to annoyance and anger. I got even angrier and I wanted to lose them, just to prove that I could, so I turned right towards Boylston Street and the subway entrance. Then I reconsidered. There were too many ways to get hurt while waiting by the side of the underground tracks where trains would rush in with little warning. Someone could push me just at the wrong moment. I shook myself. I was becoming paranoid in a really bad way. There was a better way to lose a tracker, and it was more fun, too.

A few months ago, the manager of the Hermes store on Boylston had celebrated her birthday with a party at the hotel. She had insisted on planning the event directly with the General Manager, no banquet managers for her, and during our planning session she had invited me to visit the store. Right now would be the perfect time.

The shop actually had a doorman and was empty of customers. The sales lady approached me, looking askance at my disheveled appearance. She obviously had a major discount with Hermes and was wearing a knee length black A-line skirt and a blouse with the signature curlicues of the brand while I had ceased looking like a hotel manager. I had left the jacket of my dark gray pant suit behind in my office. The cream colored blouse with long sleeves had looked respectable when I had started my walk, but I had rolled up the sleeves haphazardly in the heat of my somewhat hysterical rapid walk and the bow at the neck had come undone. I asked for Mrs. Ransome, and was rewarded with a supercilious look of doubt and an unwilling agreement to call her. Evelyne Ransome was dressed like a twin of the sales woman, but obviously had had an encounter of the worst kind with her cosmetician. Her right eyebrow had been over plucked and had a perpetual look of surprise. Worse, the left side looked normal. I tried to avoid looking at her face. Fortunately, she remembered me and her invitation. Foolishly, she had thought that the salary of a hotel manager ran to Hermes and hoped that the invitation would lead to a purchase, and I did nothing to disabuse her. I had hoped for a cup of time-consuming coffee, but with a sad look, made weird by the errant eyebrow, she told me that she had to go to a meeting outside the shop.

"But please, feel free to browse. Of course, I'll be happy to arrange a discount for anything you want."

She walked out of the store, leaving me under the now less suspicious look of the saleswoman. So I browsed. The least expensive items were the perfumes, followed at a distance of several hundred dollars by the scarves. I fingered silk blouses priced at thousands of dollars. Trying something would have been pushing it, especially for superego-ridden me. I mused to myself that had Betsy been here, she would have done it and had fun trying on clothes that cost more than she made in a week. After about twenty minutes of dedicated browsing, I hoped that any follower, unable to enter through the guarded door, would have despaired, and waving gaily, I left the store and headed for the subway entrance. In minutes I was back at the hotel.

"Where have you been?" Betsy, who had been pacing up and down the lobby floor, asked accusingly.

"I thought that I had the time for a walk, but I've just spent hours dodging Porter. He followed me all the way to the Boston Gardens."

She wrinkled her nose and squinted at me. "What are you talking about? Porter couldn't have been following you."

"Well, I didn't actually see him, but I was followed, and it must have been him," I answered indignantly to cover my feeling that perhaps I had been a bit silly.

"Porter didn't follow you. He just checked in an hour ago."

CHAPTER FIFTEEN

Betsy - Wednesday Afternoon

That was it. Just like that. I've been carrying a watermelon around inside my heart and now it's supposed to be gone. Rebecca has gone back to being my friend instead of a distant cold boss, and it's not just because she needs me to get her out of trouble. Peter knows that she didn't kill Marshall and I didn't have to tell any secrets to get him there. Everything is just peachy keen, so why do I feel so empty? The drama is missing. It was the whimper instead of the bang. There was no big scene and I couldn't help feeling that there should have been, but I can just hear Mom telling me to get on with it.

I had said that I had work to do, but the truth was that the last thing I wanted to do was check phone records and time sheets. What I really wanted to do was catch the killer, and there was something that they all had seemed to miss. If Porter killed Marshall and then went back to a room that he would have to leave every day, he would have to get rid of the gun. Walking around Boston with a concealed weapon is not a great idea and I was guessing that he stashed it somewhere in the hotel until he, not being a very experienced murderer, could figure out what to do with it. The garbage compactor might seem like a good idea, but the gun would snag something and make a hell of a noise. He knew hotels and he probably would know that. He also probably knew all the possible hiding places in a guest room where the chambermaid would never look.

The panel under the built-in closet covered an open area. I would need tools to get it off. The grill over the air-conditioning vent came off and hid a space behind it. I would need a screwdriver for that. Each room had its own fan-coil air-conditioning mechanism and it had to be accessible for repairs. The ceiling that hid it was actually made of wide panels that matched the color of the ceiling and rested on narrow rails. To get at that space I would only need a chair that would hold me.

I went down to Piotr and borrowed the tools. He didn't even ask me why I needed them, and I felt a twinge of guilt. I should have asked for his help, and he could get at those spaces faster than I could, but I wanted to do it myself.

It was crucial to call reception to make sure that if Porter turned up early, they would alert me. That done, I rushed to the room and began to search for the gun. The fan-coil was easiest, not just for me, but for him, too, so I pulled a chair over to the lower ceiling at the entrance to the room. I climbed up barefoot, to avoid marking the upholstery, and gently moved the first panel. All I could see was a lot of dust. I could shine a flashlight in to see deeper, but I wasn't tall enough, so I had to move all but the last panel. Still no gun, but there were clouds of dust that made me sneeze. The filters were scheduled for cleaning before the summer, and I told myself that I should remind Anna that the time was long gone. She would have to get a staff organized to work together with Piotr in cleaning the filters and getting rid of some of the dust. I replaced the ceiling panels carefully.

That was a delicate job. If they weren't just right, they would look off, and could even fall. Rebecca had told me about a short stint that she had done abroad, where a mild earthquake had moved a panel just enough to leave it almost in place until a guest slammed the door and had the roof fall in on her. I didn't mind the idea of Porter having the ceiling fall on him, but he might catch on to what I had done.

I pulled the chair over to the grill. It was clear that I had to be careful not to scratch the paint, and it wasn't easy. I realized that it couldn't have been easy for him either, and there were no scratch marks. I peered in with the help of the flashlight, cursed my lack of height, and jumped off the chair, heading for the built-in closet. That was hard, and I was close to calling Piotr for help when I finally succeeded in pulling the strip of veneer covered wood away. There was no gun there. Damn! It had to be there. I replaced the wood, not bothering to actually get it wedged back in. Later I could report the damage and get it fixed, but Porter would never notice.

I glanced at the room. It seemed perfect, and I quietly walked out, but as I closed the door, my cell rang. I had forgotten to put it on vibrate.

"That guest you wanted us to notify you when he checked in, well he's just checking in now."

"Oh, fuck."

"Excuse me?"

"I just wished you good luck," I lied, wincing, and muttered a thank you.

Peter wasn't here yet, but I ran down the two flights, with no patience to wait for the elevator, to get Rebecca. Milly just shook her head.

"She's not here now."

"What? Where is she? This is no joke. I need her now."

"She had to go out." Milly checked her watch. "She should be back in about an hour." She smiled at me as I gritted my teeth and marched out of the office, dialing Peter's number as I walked. At first the phone rang and rang. I kept trying. Then it went to voicemail and I cursed and dialed again. And then again. And then one last time. Finally I heard his voice filled with impatience.

"Sweetie, I can't talk now. Believe me I wouldn't do this but something not connected to this case came up, and I have to get it out of the way. I promise I'll be there in time to meet our killer when he checks in."

"He's checking in right now, as we speak." I gritted my teeth again, and listened to shocked silence.

"That was a surprise."

"You bet."

"I will get to the hotel, with reinforcements, just as soon as I can. You go nowhere near the guy. You hear?"

"I hear. Finish your whatever it is and come soon. Please." I hung up. I felt like slamming the phone down, but it wasn't really his fault, and you can't slam an iPhone. That's one of the main disadvantages of the modern digital phone. There is no replacement for the satisfaction of slamming a phone down when you're really pissed off.

I went into the lobby, but he was no longer there. I had just missed seeing the man that we had been chasing since Marshall had been killed. I began to pace back and forth.

"Betsy, you missed him." Russell, who was the receptionist working at the front desk, called out. "Do you want me to put through a call to his room?"

"No!" I snapped at him and immediately felt the need to apologize. "Sorry, Russell. I don't need to speak with him, just to know when he checks in. It's okay."

He looked at me, saw my frazzled state, and asked, "Can I bring you something from the bar? Something hot or cold?" he added with a look of sympathy, "Or something alcoholic?"

"Thanks Russ. You're a good guy. I'll get over to the bar and get something for myself. I'm waiting for Rebecca and I'm waiting for a group of policemen, too. If you see them before I do, just give me a call."

"Will do." He smiled and returned to his post in reception.

I walked quickly to the bar, grabbed a tall glass of soda, drank it down in one go, and returned to pacing the length of the lobby. Each step increased the depth of my irritation. Didn't Peter want to catch this guy? Worse, where the hell was Rebecca? She knew that he could check in any time. To be honest, I had convinced both of them that Porter always showed up much later, but when did they start believing everything I said. Saying that to myself just made me madder. I continued to pace. The floor of the lobby was marble with a blue carpet covering most of the central area. The blue was bordered with a gold pattern of fleur de lis around the edges and in a smaller square around the center where a large glass table held a massive bouquet of roses and ferns. I paced around the carpet and then on the border and then around the table. Then I paced from the large glass window to the revolving door and on the fourth round, as I approached the door, I met Rebecca coming in.

""Where have you been?" I couldn't keep the accusing tone out of my voice and saw the surprise and hurt on her face.

"I thought that I had the time for a walk, but I've just spent hours dodging Porter. He followed me all the way to the Boston Gardens. I was pretty shook up."

What the hell was she talking about? "Porter couldn't have been following you."

"Well, I didn't actually see him, but I was followed, and it must have been him," she answered indignantly.

"Porter didn't follow you. He just checked in an hour ago."

CHAPTER SIXTEEN

Rebecca - Wednesday Afternoon

The news that Porter was already in the hotel was a thunderbolt. If he was here, who had followed me? Had anyone actually followed me? Was I totally losing it? If he was in the hotel, had I missed it all? I questioned Betsy with trepidation. I wanted it all to be over and at the same time I wanted to be in on it.

"Oh, no. Is Peter here? Did he get him?"

"He should be here. But he got held up. I'm waiting here for him. He's not gonna let me go anywhere near the action, but you can. He'll never think to look for you. I have the perfect way to let you share in what's going down."

"I'm not completely sure that I want to share in anything 'going down'." I framed my words with fingered quotation marks. "I want to be involved, but after my noon walk, I am less and less interested in any heroics."

"Sure you are, just as long as they are the very safe kind of heroics. I just happen to know that the room next to Porter's has been out if order for a few days with some kind of plumbing problem and is marked as double locked by Piotr so that Peter will be told that he can't get in."

"That can't be. I don't know anything about a work order there."

She looked at me with mounting exasperation until suddenly I understood.

"Marshall isn't the only one who knows how to manipulate the truth with a computer to change fact with fiction."

"Will he fall for it?"

"Anyone would fall for it. It looks real and that's what reception will tell him, but you have to go there, and you have to go now. Peter will be here any minute, I hope."

I made a face. My adventure on the Comm Ave Mall had kept me from lunch, and I had not even received the expected little cookies and coffee at Hermes.

"I'll go right now, but you have to send a waiter with a sandwich. I'm starving."

"I'll bring the sandwich as long as Peter doesn't show up. But we have to be quick, so run."

I ran, ignoring the feeling that I had been manipulated right along with the computer program, and reaching the door of the room next to Porter's, quickly opened the lock with my master key. If the room had actually been put out of order, it would have been double-locked to keep the cleaners out, but, of course, the door opened normally. I closed it quietly behind me and walked over to the armchair by the window. Fortunately, I had come so quickly that I still had the backpack pocketbook that I had brought for the pleasant walk that I had planned. I always leave my Kindle in my pocketbook. Waiting is never a problem if I have the Kindle, no matter what causes the delay. The only problem, I knew, is that if the book is a good one I tend to become totally absorbed and oblivious to what goes on around me. I had to force myself to read with half an eye. Even so, I became absorbed in my book and lost track of time until my stomach growled. I wondered where Betsy was. I hoped that she would have the time to scare me up a sandwich. The bar would prepare it happily, and if she let them think that it was for her, they would even prepare it quickly. Then I heard the door knob twist, and I stood up and walked to the door in ravenous anticipation. The door edged open. A pink polyester expanse of stomach walked in, followed by the rest of him. Shocked, I had no doubt that I was looking at Anderson Porter. Once balding, he was now almost completely bald and a few straggling hairs attempted a futile comb over on top of a florid round face. Once overweight, he was now a fat man. He began to open the door of the built-in closet next to the entrance, before becoming aware that he was not alone.

"I'm so sorry. This room was empty and they let me store something in the closet." His eyes widened and his mouth gaped. "I know who you are. You're the manager here. I'll just take my luggage and get out of your way."

I had no doubt that the gun he had used to kill Marshall had been hidden in the closet. If he got it and ran, Peter would have missed catching him with the best evidence in the world in his hand, and I stupidly, and without thinking things out, flew at the open closet and the black Samsonite carry-on that had been hidden there. For a fat man, he moved very quickly, and he lunged at me. We collapsed in a heap on the floor, both if us clutching at parts of the suitcase. I was pinned under several hundred pound of murderer, and I could barely squeak out a feeble 'Help!' If he got to the gun first, he would probably use it on me and that made me even more desperate. I again tried to squawk out a cry for help, but a pink wall had collapsed on me and was squeezing out my breath. There was nothing left for screaming. I had not done a lot of advance planning when I tackled an enormous killer, and now blind terror washed over me for the few seconds before the door opened again and Peter appeared with his new detective. They grabbed at Porter and soon had his arms pinned behind him, but he was still half on top of me, squeezing out what little breath I had left. It took the two of them to lift him away from me and they struggled with his resistant weight. Fortunately for me, Detective Joiner was stronger than he looked and finally I could breath, albeit asthmatically.

"What is going on?" Porter gasped, struggling with my two saviors. "Get away from me. Are all you people crazy? I'm calling the police."

"We are the police. Who are you?" Joiner asked gruffly.

"I work here," he began, and then, glancing at me, he shifted his story. "I work for the hotel chain. Just let me go and I'll show you identification."

"First tell us what you're doing here." Peter was still breathing hard from the struggle.

"I have permission from the head of reception to store a few things here. I'm a guest."

"I thought you said you worked here."

"You're just trying to confuse me. Just ask Marshall Hammersmith. He runs reception here. Ask her, she'll tell you," he added, pointing at me.

"That would be a bit difficult," I whispered, not sure if I was allowed to talk or if I was going to be part of the arrest in any way aside for my being a wrestling mat.

"We're going to finish this discussion at the station." Peter had recovered from the strenuous capture, and he wanted his killer locked safely away.

I had hoped that they would continue to ask questions where I could hear. I had my doubts about how much it really mattered to me in the final analysis. Being almost crushed to death had given me a different sense of proportion, but still, I was sure that being involved was important. That was about to slip out of my fingers, and there was nothing I could do.

"Why? I didn't do anything. Okay, maybe Marshall let me stay a few extra nights without registering, but I'll pay. It's just that the chain won't let us comp staff for more than two nights without a manager's signature." He stole a quick look at me. "She'll tell you. We should have gotten the signature but it was last minute. I had a family wedding here and I had a few extra days off to come earlier. Just ask Marshall. He'll tell you. He knows the whole story. He'll tell you I was gonna pay. I'll get my wallet out and pay you now."

The two detectives looked at each other, and Peter nodded to his temporary partner.

"I don't think that Mr. Hammersmith will be able to confirm your story. Did you actually think he would be doing that after you shot him in the head?"

"I didn't shoot anyone. I don't even have a gun. Shoot anyone? Shoot Marshall, you mean? Marshall? Someone shot Marshall? Is he okay?" He looked at the two grim police detectives in confusion. "Is Marshall okay? Is he alive? No! No, it can't be."

Before they could stop him, he tore away from the detectives and plopped down suddenly on the bed. Without any warning, he began to cry. We all looked at each other and then at the huge man blubbering as he half sat, half lay on the bed. It was at that moment that Betsy, carrying a tray with a plate on it walked in. I saw the sandwich and grabbed at it.

"What on earth is going on?"

Peter looked at her and answered gruffly, "What are you doing here? Aren't you supposed to be somewhere else?"

"I'm just bringing my boss a sandwich, as requested, and you're not answering me."

I quickly came to her defense, "She's just doing what I asked. You're just in time to meet Anderson Porter." I held out my hand and pointed at the huge pink and chino clad man who continued to sob but with less gusto.

"So this is the man who's been stealing our rooms since Sunday night and who killed our reservation manager on Monday. Has he confessed yet?"

Despite the noise he was making, Porter was listening to her. "I may have been here since Sunday night, but I didn't kill Marshall or anyone else. I sat with him on Sunday night right here in the room and then he left. He left in very good condition. He said he was planning a few hours of sleep and then he had an early morning date with a chick. You have your security cameras in the hallways. Just check."

"You have security cams in the hallways?" Peter bellowed at Betsy. "Why didn't anyone tell me?"

"You never asked and we never thought it could be important," I answered for Betsy who was on her way out the door. "I think that my security officer just went to check."

Peter focused on Porter again who was now sniffling. "I want him out of here. I want to ask him what he knows about Marshall's date, assuming that his story is true, and I want to do it at the station.

"You can't arrest me. I haven't done anything."

I'm not arresting you, yet, just asking questions, but sure I can hold you. Try petty theft."

"Not so petty," I interrupted. "From what I've been checking, for the number of years he's been at it, with New York City rates for most of it, he's probably managed to get away with at least a quarter of a million dollars."

They all looked at me. Peter and Joiner were shocked and Porter was horrified to find out that his activities were no longer secret.

"Harold, take him in."

"If he doesn't want to go, I'm gonna need reinforcements."

"Oh, I think he'll cooperate now. If he helps us with our murder case, we could do our best to help him with his grand larceny."

"All right, all right, but you'll see that Marshall left around one thirty in the morning and I never left the rooms until seven or eight the next morning. When was he killed?"

Peter had no intention of answering, and he seemed to ignore Porter, who continued with even greater desperation.

"He was my best friend. Why should I kill him? He said he had a morning shift and that he arranged to start early because he had a rendezvous. He even said that he had a meeting with a woman who wanted something from him and that that way he would be able to get what he wanted from her. He sort of smirked. He was pretty happy."

Betsy returned with a grim look. She was holding a disc and she gave it to Peter.

"I made a copy for you. He's telling the truth, damn it. He came into the room dragging a big carry-on behind him at around seven-thirty. Marshall finished his shift at eleven, and he showed up here just a few minutes later. He left at around one-thirty in the morning. They even had the gall to order room-service."

Porter had been listening just as hard as we were and he added a few words. "That was just a few beers and some munchies."

"Thank you." Betsy turned to face him and answered with sarcasm dripping from her voice. "If the story about a woman is true." She paused.

"It's true, I swear. Maybe some woman killed him."

"Ya think? Now the perp is helping us with the investigation. How nice," Peter added.

Betsy was intent on continuing. "If some unidentified woman met with Marshall in his office and killed him or saw the killer, we have to find her and that seems impossible. We don't know who she is, what she looks like, how old she is, what she wanted. What he wanted, we can guess. We are back to square one."

"Betsy, love, there is no we, remember? We have other directions to check, and now that we've gotten this nonsense out of the way, we're going to do just that."

He took out his phone, punched in the number of the station, and told Jake to get started on plan B.

"If that was plan A, what was I?" I pouted.

"You? That was working by the book, no insult intended." He pointed at Porter. "Joiner, get him out of here."

Porter stood and meekly allowed himself to be handcuffed. The two officers of the law left with their still sniffling captive, leaving Betsy and me.

I sat down on the ruffled bed and moved my arms and legs up and down, testing to make sure nothing was permanently damaged. "It's not so bad. We do have a few possibilities."

"Oh?"

"Marshal was having a thing with the new receptionist."

"Get out of here. No way. Someone was pulling your leg."

I tried not to let the feeling that I had just been insulted show in my voice. I know that Betsy thought that nobody ever told me anything real, because I was the boss, and there is a lot of truth in that. Nobody was going to confide in the very person who could fire them, but I wasn't blind.

"Nobody pulled my leg. I found out when I saw in the computer records how Marshall was covering up for her mistakes. Marshall never covered for anyone without getting something in return."

"No 'never speak ill of the dead' for you."

"We're not writing his obituary, we're trying to find his killer, and he was a genuine creep. Anyway, I talked to Lydia and she confessed."

"Lydia killed him!"

"No, of course not. She confessed to a sort of half-hearted affair. Well, half-hearted on his part. She was really in to it."

"She told you that? Wow. I am impressed. I thought that the boss, by definition, is the last to know."

"No big deal. She was pretty pathetic, and she was no big deal for Marshall either. He never even bothered to cover his tracks, because he knew that the minute someone caught on, she was toast. And someone would have caught on. Me or Jeri, for starters. She was so bad at the job. She was a walking disaster, but she has no, I don't know exactly what to call it, she has no maneuvers. I don't think she did it."

"Did what? Are you changing subjects?"

"No. The murder. She just didn't have it in her and she was really besotted with him. We should check her out, but she didn't do it."

"We should check her out? You mean us, not them? I notice that you didn't share this tidbit with the detective who is madly in love with me."

"You heard him. There is no 'we' with us in it, so you and I will just have to make a new 'we'."

"You said that we have a few possibilities. Who else?"

"It could be someone we don't know about. Marshall was not a nice man. That seems the most likely to me because he could have damaged all kinds of people, but it could also be his wife."

"Whose wife?"

"Marshall's wife. She was here, looking for papers that he had."

"What?" Betsy was flabbergasted. "He wasn't married."

"Apparently he was."

She opened her mouth to respond, but remained wordless with a look of shock until she began to calculate.

"We can look for her among the people who came in that morning. I gave the disc to Peter but it's saved on the computer."

"Well I didn't actually see her face, only her angry back when she couldn't get what she wanted, but Milly saw her."

I saw a serious look wash over Betsy's face at the thought that we would have to involve yet another person in our machinations.

"The reason we should give this to Peter is still the same as it was before. They can do it better. They can find her and we can't."

"I thought you were pissed at him for shutting us out."

"I am. I was, but I'll talk to him again when there's no audience. We have to give this to him."

I threw up my hands in disgust, because she was right, and I had a closing banquet for our barmen's convention to handle.

CHAPTER SEVENTEEN

Betsy - Wednesday Evening

I dragged myself up the three flights of stairs to our apartment. The building is old, and has no elevator, but the rooms are large and the ceilings high, so I often blessed our luck in finding it. The little side street next to the Fenway is close enough for us to walk the Fens often and far enough away that the traffic was only a dull roar. Even exhausted as I was, I still was able to look around and enjoy what we had done to the place. The wooden floors that we had sanded and varnished were gleaming and the windows that had only a view of other apartment buildings were decorated with small glass balls of soft colors in the living room and shaded by long moss green curtains in our bedroom. We had furnished mainly with giveaways from our parents and with finds from antique shops that we had discovered on trips around New England. I loved the tiny drop-leaf desk where I had left some really good books, and the green sofa was inviting, but I had no time to sit down. I had work to do before I would be in condition to do a number on Peter. I felt sweaty and I would have to spruce up. A shower would be a good start, followed by a cloud of perfume and the most subtle make-up that I knew how to apply. Then I opened a bottle of wine, put candlesticks with long white tapers on the table and lit them. The next step was to order Chinese take-away from Peter's favorite Chinese restaurant. The food had to be timed to arrive five minutes before he did, and I could calculate that with the help of a judicious call to my buddy, the dispatcher at the station. Mata Hari type seduction wasn't exactly my strong suit, but it was worth a try.

Everything ordered and prepared, I looked at my watch and saw that if the traffic wasn't too bad, he would arrive in the five minutes I would use to sit, relax and read the paper, at least the headlines. Then the phone rang. Except for annoying telemarketers, my mother was the only person I knew who used the regular phone to call me. If it was someone selling me an electric blanket or a time-share, I would hang up. If they were offering a retirement home, I might take them up on it. It was Mom.

"How are you, love?" Not even leaving a space for the noncommittal answer that was safest, she carried on. "Since you were here for dinner, I've had to get my information from Marloo to know what's going on with you."

"Marloo? Marloo, the baker or Marloo the lawyer?"

She laughed. "A bit of both, I guess. You never told me that Rebecca was arrested."

"Rebecca wasn't arrested. She just was questioned and she's completely in the clear, and how did you know? How did Marloo know?"

"I knew just because."

"Just because what?"

"Just because of Mr. Robertson. You remember Mr. Robertson who runs the fish market. Well, his son just graduated from the police academy, and he was just leaving the station after his shift, and he was talking on his cell phone to his dad. His son calls his father at least once a day, unlike some sons and daughters I could mention."

I began to tune her out while she gave me a well deserved lecture, but then it got interesting.

My mother, as usual, could tell that I was no longer listening so, in a heartbeat, she cut off her complaints.

"You should be paying attention. He, the son, knows Rebecca because she buys fish at his dad's place."

I gritted my teeth and looked at my watch.

"He saw Peter bringing Rebecca in. He knows Peter because of you. Well, he was on the phone already, and I was buying fish. He got in some really nice cod, and it's so hard to find now."

She was doing it on purpose. Nobody dithers less than my mother, but she was punishing me, and I took it because it was deserved. She had tried to help me and she had tried to help Rebecca, and all she wanted in exchange was to be kept in the loop. How could I blame her for wanting the same thing that I wanted? So I sighed in resignation and flowed with it.

"How did Marloo know?"

"She knew, because I told her. She's a very good lawyer, appearances aside, and I knew that Rebecca would need her. So I called and asked her if she could get right down to the station, and she did. I also know that Rebecca's off the hook now. I know because Marloo told me, and she found out because the police hate having her in their hair, and the minute they could eliminate Rebecca, they told her. She probably knew before Rebecca knew."

I discovered that I was holding my breath, and I let it out with a whoosh that Mom heard. She laughed, and I knew that, at least for now, I was off the hook, too.

"Betsy, I know a little less about how you are, and that matters to me much much more. You've been having a strained time with your boss, who also happens to be Rebecca and who is also like a daughter to me, so what's happening? Has this mess made it better or worse?"

"You are one smart lady, Mom. Somehow it's made it better. At first, maybe, because she needed my help in something that was personal, but it, like, broke the ice."

"I'm happy to hear that, not just for you, but for her. She is such a lonely person."

"Rebecca lonely? She has a million friends and a great marriage."

"She has a million acquaintances who admire her because they want something from her, and her marriage works as well as it does because she works a thirteen hour day and because most of the time Jason is abroad building a bridge in the middle of some jungle or digging a mine in the middle of some desert. Rebecca is the loneliest person I know. I realize that you and Peter have no idea how important your friendship is for her. Even Rebecca may have no idea."

I was stunned into silence. This was something that deserved more thought, but not now.

"Mom, I gotta run. Peter will be home any minute. I'm planning to sweet talk him into letting us share more of the investigation. That 'us' includes Rebecca and you, too. Mom, I love you."

"Bets, I love you, too."

I hung up and immediately heard his key in the door, I busied myself putting boxes of his favorite dishes on the table and organizing chopsticks for beginning the meal, and forks for when he decided he had had enough of authenticity. I welcomed him with an embrace and a lingering kiss, and he responded with a roaring laugh.

"No subtle advances, huh? Right to it. I know exactly what you want."

"And the answer is 'no', huh?" I stepped away from him and stuck out my tongue.

"The answer is, tell me why you think I should agree, without resorting to childish gestures. I know that if you think I should let you cooperate with us, you have a good reason, aside from that you just want it. I want to hear the reason."

"I really want to be involved. It's my hotel."

He laughed. "And?"

"This has a lot to do with the hotel world. A lot of the clues are hotel world clues. Rebecca and I know that world. We know stuff that could help you, and it would work better if we were really involved. We speak the language." I figured that the time to mention the wife was after he agreed.

He smiled seductively. "If I agree, what's in it for me, personally, I mean."

"Rebecca isn't into that kind of thing, and Jason is bigger than you, and I would kill you."

He grinned, and I knew we were in.

"Thanks, sweetie. We'll behave ourselves, I promise. As proof, I can already give you information. Did you know that Marshall had a secret unhappy wife?"

"Betsy, love, that is the first place we looked. It's usually someone close to the victim. We put it on the back burner because of all the proof of joint hanky panky with Anderson Porter. That was Plan B. By the way, I have a bit of hotel gossip for Rebecca. Her colleague in Manhattan had a hysterical fit when we told him about his front office manager. He's scared to death that Hanley will fire him when he finds out how much money Porter stole."

"I'll tell her. She should get a bonus for discovering it and stopping it. I gather that Jake got a lot of information about the wife. Did he know that she was in the hotel?"

Peter opened his mouth to retort and closed it. All that came out was a strangled "Umph"

"You'll have to get more information from Rebecca and from Milly. She's the one who actually met the woman."

"All right. All right. I am convinced."

"I hear a 'but'."

"A big one. Whoever killed Marshall is a dangerous person who thinks he or she got away with it. Let's assume it was the wife. What do you think she'll do to keep anyone from finding out?"

"Anything."

"Right. Anything. If she discovers that you and your boss are snooping, she will act. Let me do the snooping."

"What about your danger?"

"I am bigger than you. I am stronger than you. I have a partner who covers my back, and I have a gun."

"I have a partner."

He chortled. "Yeah, right. I gather that things are okay again with your partner."

"Thank goodness. It was really weighing me down. What's funny is that my Mom was more concerned about Rebecca. She said that Rebecca was really lonely. Isn't that weird?"

"It makes a lot of sense. It comes with the job."

"Why do you say that?"

"Because I see it on the force, too. It's a hierarchy, just like the hotel business. The higher you go, the fewer friends you can have. The captain used to be one of us and he was a regular guy. He isn't now. He can't be while he's running the show. Some of them on the job resent it, but I just feel sorry for him. Well he got something in exchange, but I wouldn't want it, even for the power and the money."

Now I was wordless. I had somehow vaguely known that that was the way Peter thought, but it had never been put into words. Way back when we had just begun to get serious about each other, I had been frightened by the potential for grief in being a cop's girlfriend, but I had never ever thought that he would give it up to sit at a safe desk. That was part of the package. When we got married it was going to be my concern and it would never change. So I said nothing, just smiled and kissed him.

One kiss led to another, and more kisses led to more than kisses. Within minutes, most of our clothing was draped on various pieces of furniture around us and the wide, worn, cushioned, green, velvet couch that we had found at a garage sale once again proved itself a useful purchase.

What seemed like hours later, Peter suggested a walk on the Fenway. I just groaned and the subject was closed. Then with great hunger, we ate the gelid, greasy, tasty food.

"Speaking of friendship..."

"Oh, was that was that was?"

We both laughed.

"When do you plan to tell your mother? Until you tell her, I can't tell my parents, because the minute my mom hangs up the phone, she'll be dialing the number of the Connolly Family residence, and I really do want to tell them."

"When we have a definite date, I'll tell her. I promise. Not a definite date, but an approximate date, because we have to make sure the church is free."

"Okay, my love, then how about the coming September as a not definite date?"

My breath stuck in my throat. This was even more than a marriage proposal. This was the real thing down to the wire, and I could not conceive of living without this man. I began to cry.

Peter looked at me in horror, and when I saw his face I realized that he thought that I was backing out.

"Peter, you idiot, these are tears of happiness. September is a wonderful idea. We'd already planned to take vacation and do some traveling, so we both have time off, and instead of a regular trip, we can have the honeymoon we talked about before all this mess started. I'll call Father Tim in the morning to get a date and I'll swear him to silence until we can tell our families."

We had long ago talked about the religious thing, so thank God that was not an issue. Peter's folks were sort of nothing, both born to vaguely Unitarian families, but they were, fortunately, cool with the fact that I would have to marry in our local church, and that our kids would be baptized in the same church. A lot of my school friends were lapsed, and, I guess, so was I, but Bridget was Bridget, and she was very Irish Catholic.

I am constantly reminded of a joke she told on herself and her commitments to her faith. She would put on her deepest brogue and tell about the beautiful Irish girl who left the country, moved to Birmingham in England and, not finding a job, finally became a hooker, and a very successful one at that. She regularly sent money to her mother, but was hesitant to return home. Finally she yielded to her mum's constant begging for her to visit, and she booked the trip. As she walked up the main street of the village, she met her mum coming out of the local pub. Overwhelmed by guilt, she hugged her mother, and began a stammered confession of why she hadn't visited home before.

'Mum, I love you, and I wanted to come but I was embarrassed.'

'Love, why should you be embarrassed?'

'Haven't you ever questioned how I was able to send you so much money? I, I, have, that is, I have become a pro..'

The old lady fainted dead away.

Frightened and guilty, the girl ran into the pub and brought out a glass of water that she splashed on her mother who slowly came to.

"What did you just say, girl?'

'I said that I'd become a prostitute.'

She sighed in relief. 'Oh, thank God. I thought I heard ya say that you'd become a Protestant'.

It must have somewhat after one in the morning when Peter's phone rang. When his phone rang so late, it usually meant someone was dead. That was so sobering that I never ever complained. I began to get up and make him a cup of coffee, but he grabbed my hand and signaled me to wait.

"Jake, do you know what time it is?" He paused to hear an apology. "Well I am glad you couldn't sleep, so that when they called you, you didn't have to be awakened. What is so urgent about a break-in in an apartment in Quincy of all places? That's not even close to Boston."

He listened carefully and suddenly sat up straight.

"Christ, you're right. I'll get right over there. If I need back-up I'll call the station."

"Peter, what's going on? Why do you have to go to Quincy?"

"I'm not going to Quincy. There was a break-in in an apartment there, and the beat cop, bless him, remembered that the Quincy PD had been asked to check that apartment for us. The contact was Jake so he called him, despite the hour. It was Marshall's place."

"I remember that he lived somewhere out of the city. He used to complain about the commute and used to beg Rebecca to okay an overnight in the hotel whenever he had a late shift. I never thought of Quincy. That really is far. Why would anyone break in there? Maybe it's just a coincidence."

"I don't believe in coincidence. The place was really torn up, but what was mostly flung about was paper. Documents. He had a desk in a small guest bedroom and it was literally taken apart. If someone was looking for some document, and didn't find it, wouldn't he go to the hotel next? Do you guys leave personal documents there?"

"Sure. It's the best place, if you have an office there. Beats stacking papers under the bed."

"I have to go check it out."

"I'm coming with you."

"No you're not. There's no need. Anyway it may really be a coincidence."

"You don't believe in coincidence, and neither do I, but it will be much easier if I come. I have all the keys. I know all the places. You need me there."

"Don't you have one of your security people there all night?"

I snorted and began to get dressed. The drive through the silent city took only minutes despite the fact that there was still quite a bit of traffic, and I wondered what all those people were doing up so late. Reaching the hotel, we drove around to the back underground entrance to the parking garage. I used my card to open the gate, and we drove in. The garage was almost empty. Nearly all of the convention goers had flown into Boston and had no need to rent cars because all of the trips were organized with buses. Rebecca's green Volvo was still parked in her regular spot.

"They must still be carrying on with the final banquet. She won't leave until the cleanup is almost done."

"Wow. That's punishment for the boss. Always?"

"We take turns. There's supposed to be a banquet manager, but the last one quit when she had a baby. She couldn't handle the hours. We're still looking."

"No wonder. Seems like a lot of your managers are having babies. Is it contagious or an occupational hazard that we will have to remember?"

We both laughed and I felt myself blush.

The elevator rose slowly and smoothly from the garage to the lobby floor. We stepped out to a feeling of emptiness and silence. Russell was behind the reception desk and he waved at us with a puzzled expression. He didn't ask me what we were doing there so late, and that was for the best, because I didn't think that I wanted to tell him.

The ballroom was clean. The tables were stacked in a corner and next to them were several towers of stacked banqueting chairs. The white covers for the chairs, the dirty tablecloths and the napkins were tied in big bulky rolls waiting for the laundry to come and take them in the morning. The podium had been pushed into a corner. The room was silent and empty.

We tried Rebecca's office. It was locked and dark.

CHAPTER EIGHTEEN

Rebecca - Wednesday Night

Being a banquet manager is not something I ever really wanted to do. The hours are awful with early mornings to meet with potential clients and nights that sometimes seemed endless. Because of the long hours, the pay is usually very good, but not good enough. Some of the clients were easy and cooperative. Some were nice but demanding, but every so often there was a bride from hell. Once, I even told a couple that they should go elsewhere since it was obvious that nothing we could do could possibly be satisfactory. They panicked and became almost nice. So you may ask what I was doing here at night managing a closing banquet for a group of convention guests who had spent most of their time in Boston being tipsy at best and totally smashed at worst. We had a wonderful banquet manager, Iris Vandyke, until last year. Two years ago she got married. The ceremony and party was in the hotel and we gave her the best wedding that we could. Then she got pregnant. Then she had a beautiful baby girl and took several months off. When she came back, it was to tell us that she could not continue. She wanted to spend more time with her baby and more time with her husband and it just would not work out. Since then we have been looking for a replacement, and since then all of the department managers have been taking turns covering for her. I didn't realize what a bargain she had been and I had just about resigned myself to offering a much higher salary, but in any case, there was a banquet tonight and it was my turn.

It was still early, but I could check the ballroom, just in case. I knew that I could count on the housekeeping and the banqueting staff, but that was partly because they knew I would check.

The lights had still not been lit, so that was the first thing I did. I preferred to keep the lights a bit low. It seemed to create a quieter atmosphere. I lit the pewter wall sconces and the three main chandeliers. I tried several rows of the small ceiling lights, looked around, and turned them off. There was enough light. Fortunately our Revere Ballroom showed not a trace of the fire, and I breathed a sigh of relief. The understated elegance of the walls of wide dusty light blue stripes alternating with cream, and the dark blue carpet with circles of flowers was ready for the onslaught. The larger part of the hall was set up for dining with large tables each for ten guests scattered through the room, and the smaller part formed a foyer where the guests would enjoy a cocktail reception before the dinner. The guests would enter the main hall from the side, through the foyer after imbibing yet more alcohol, and would face a small stage with a podium for the various speakers. The banner of the Barmen's Association, featuring the association's logo, was hung behind the podium, and when I saw it, I gaped open-mouthed. I suddenly realized why the reservation department of the previous owners of the hotel had taken the group. The name was written on three rows and the word 'Bar' was the largest and most prominent. I would have to grudgingly forgive them for the wild, unfounded, irrational assumption that we had the size and facilities to host the Bar Association convention. I giggled as I pushed open the doors leading into the kitchen, where, despite the early hour, there was already quiet hysteria.

The cooks were busy chopping, cutting, steaming, and whatever they had to do. They were all furiously busy but they were still keeping a constant eye on the chef who was standing by his desk in his little glass enclosed office, yelling into his cellphone and pulling at his hair until he resembled the sun god with peaks of hair in every direction.

I gingerly approached until he could see me, and then he suddenly stopped yelling and thrust the phone at me.

"You tell them. I ordered twenty pounds of chanterelles and the idiots sent two. Tell them that a two and a zero mean twenty, and that I have a first course to prepare with the missing damn mushrooms and I need them now," he shouted.

I tried, of course, but it was obvious that there was no way to get the missing mushrooms in time.

"Richard, please sit down and take a deep breath so that we can figure out what to do."

Unexpectedly, he sat, probably in shock at my calling him by name instead of 'chef'. I had used the French pronunciation, as he preferred, although I was well aware that he had been born and brought up as Rick Lemon and that the name had morphed into Richard Lemoine after he came back from a course at the Cordon Blue in Paris. I almost always followed tradition, and I knew that it pleased him when I called him 'chef' and when I asked permission to enter the kitchen.

"We have a few options. You can decide. I can try to change the printed menu, and if I fail, I'll get Milly back here to do it. Or, we can ignore the printed menu. I have my doubts that most of these barmen will even be able to read in their diminished capacity."

That earned me a chuckle.

"Or, if you have a quantity of regular champignon mushrooms..."

He jumped in, curious. "Of course I do."

"Chop them or fry them or whatever you want to do with them. Cut the chanterelles in quarters so that the flower shaped cap still shows on each strip and use the strips, one to a plate as a decoration. The taste will be different, but they will never know, and it will be 'filet of trout with chanterelle mushrooms' for real."

He opened his mouth to argue, thought better of it, and in mid thought, changed his mind and nodded happily. Whew. Another kitchen crisis averted.

"Rebecca, my dear, I must give instructions to the 'gard-manger' cooks, but that will take only a minute, and then I would like to take you on a tour of tonight's menu, the menu that you have helped me save."

I followed him out of the office and noticed that all the cooks were busy and studiously not looking at us. The level of tension had dropped several degrees, but not to zero because before a major banquet with a complicated menu, there was always the tension of making sure that everything was on track. Things were normal again.

We began at the 'gard-manger' where all the vegetables were cut and prepared, and the salads and cold appetizers were kept. Here, the mushrooms would be chopped and the few chanterelles sliced into lengthwise strips.

The soup was to be a pumpkin and squash mix, and it was ready for garnishing with finely cut chives. The chef took a spoon out of his pocket, dipped it into the soup and tasted. He smiled with approval, and offered me a sip. I was actually honored, because he had never done that before. His tasting spoon was his most important piece of equipment, or so he said, and he, up till now, had reserved it for himself. With a mental wish that the heat of the soup would kill any bacteria he might be carrying, I sipped. It was good, really good, and I nodded, wisely.

We carried on to the main course preparations. The duck for the duck à l'orange had already been roasted, and was being divided into portions.

"I will serve a light lemon sorbet between the soup and the duck, eh?"

"Very good, chef."

"This will be a meal far better than they deserve, but you never know."

"What is the dessert? The menu said 'Chef's Surprise'. That's the pastry chef?"

"That is because I will surprise even myself. I have petit-four sized cubes of chocolate cake, and strawberries and raspberries and blueberries, and vanilla cream and some chocolate syrup and some cream to whip and we will put it all together in a cocktail glass and it will be quite wonderful. I do the dessert because Donny caught some kind of a bug at his family party, and didn't come back to work yet, but don't you worry."

"I am definitely not worried, and I am very happy that you have solved the mushroom dilemma," I said with a straight face. "Are you sure Donny's okay? Perhaps I should pick up the phone and call him?"

"No, thanks. It's probably unnecessary." He answered too quickly. "Donny's a rock. He's been making great desserts here since even before I came."

"Uh huh. By the way, remember when we changed the purchasing system? You were trying to teach people on your staff how to do the costing. That's really a great way of doing staff training. Have you been able to continue?"

"Not really. It sort of fizzled out." He was squirming and trying hard not to make it noticeable.

"Was Donny in that program?"

"I don't really remember. It wasn't just one person. He may have been involved, but I've forgotten."

"Uh huh. A different subject before I have to run. May I make a personal request?"

"But of course."

"Do you think that I have ever interfered too much in your purchasing decisions?"

"That is a question, not a request, but the answer is no. Even when you came and asked, no, told me, that I must check price quotes, it was only doing what I know to be right."

"My request is that, when Mr. Hanley returns from his trip, and asks you about it, that you tell him what you just told me."

"With great pleasure. If Mr. Hanley is making difficulties for you because of the kitchen, I am truly sorry."

He bowed and I left the kitchen, through the dining area with all the tables, straight through to the area set up as a foyer for the reception.

I was just in time. The convention guests began to arrive in twos and threes. The three convention organizers, with whom I had dealt from the beginning, joined the flow. I greeted them, and chatted with them as the eddies became a high tide. Even the obnoxious one was on his best behavior. I imagine that they, too, were relieved that it would soon be over with no disasters.

The organizers looked the part, dressed in black tuxedos with a red carnation pinned on the lapel. Two of them looked like the Mutt and Jeff of the comic books of long ago, and I still could not remember their names. One was tall and skinny with a bushy mustache. His partner, the obnoxious one, was short and fat and also had a bushy mustache. The third one was nondescript. He looked like a store window dummy dressed in formal attire. I couldn't remember his name either. The normal dress of the convention guests during all the previous days of the convention was tee shirts and jeans. For the banquet, they were all wearing suits and a few were also in tuxedos. Normally, when we host a convention in the hotel, I try to spend time talking with the guests. I often find out how we are doing and sometimes, to my chagrin, I find out more than I want to know, but this week had been anything but normal. The only one of them I knew was Mr. Riley, and I had gotten to know him a bit more intimately than either of us would have wanted when I help him get into his room. I saw him in a corner talking to another guest, and I made a u-turn to avoid him.

The hall was filled to capacity, in fact it seemed to be filled to more than capacity, and I began to worry. Something was wrong with our count. I knew how many were staying in the hotel. There were a few invited guests, but not many because, although we had taken a fairly reasonable price for the meal, the convention organizers had bumped it up significantly, and they were the ones who actually charged. The result was that almost none of the convention guests had invited guests of their own to the banquet. Almost all of them were barmen, not bar-women and there were a lot of elegantly dressed women in the foyer. Few of them looked like anyone's wife.

We hadn't really checked guest rooms at the other meals because they all wore convention tags, but we would have to organize a checker really fast. That turned out to be easy. I saw one of the waiters passing through, and I recognized him as an erstwhile checker, and grabbed his arm. It was easy to recognize him because of his extreme height, and I remembered that he was super efficient and good at the job. He had become a waiter, instead, because of the tips. He took my orders to set up a desk to check everyone going in to eat, but that would not be enough. If the chef had enough food to feed the extras, we could set up more tables and have the receptionist take payment and give vouchers, but it was a big 'if'. I rushed to the kitchen and found the chef standing in the 'gard-manger' kitchen supervising the creation of chanterelles out of common mushrooms.

"Chef, tell me, what would happen if we added, say another twenty guests."

"No problem."

"And if it were thirty or forty?"

He stared at me. "Rebecca, have you taken leave of your senses?"

"No, but I may, soon. It seems that an indeterminate number of our convention goers have invited their own guests without reserving or paying or even bothering to tell us. If you can handle it, we can charge them and let them in. If you can't, then we'll handle that, too."

"Okay. First of all, charge the hell out of them. That should reduce the numbers a bit. They'll all get slivers of chanterelles instead of slices, and if it gets really bad, we have roast chicken in the freezer. We'll zap them in the microwave, cut them up, and serve 'poulet a l'orange." He sighed and looked me.

"Go for it. I'll have a count for you in a few minutes."

I returned to the foyer and tried vainly to find the organizers. Returning to the passageway between the foyer and the dining hall, I grabbed my tall waiter again.

"Ramon, there are a bunch of people in tuxedos, wearing red carnations in their lapels and they're probably together. Do you see them?"

It took him only a few seconds to point them out and after thanking him, I plowed through the mass of people to them.

I sighed before beginning to explain the situation. I began to understand that their job in handling all the convention participants could not have been a picnic.

"There are far more people here that what was ordered. A lot of your people are bringing in unauthorized guests. Could you please grab the mike and explain that they will have to pay at the desk to get a voucher that will get them into dinner. The meal will cost sixty-five dollars for any non-resident guest, not booked through the convention office, and they will have to also pay, hmm, let's see, an additional twenty for the reception."

"That should thin the ranks," sarcastically muttered the one of the organizers that I called Mutt.

The announcement was followed by pandemonium, and after quite a lot of bustle and noise, many of the people in the hall seemed to melt away.

Eventually, I was able to inform the chef of an additional ten diners. That was only one extra table which was already set up anyway behind a curtain for emergencies.

They all filed into the dining hall, each one giving his room number to Ramon who had provided himself with a list from reception. They milled around, finding seats, and finally sat down. One of the tuxedo-clad men marched to the podium and began to speak.

"You all know me and I assume that you all voted for me."

The audience laughed

"I will be the best president you ever had, but I'm no good at public speaking, so I'll talk now. If I wait till after you eat, I'll have to talk to an empty room."

More laughter.

"My speech will be about our antecedents. Before I was elected, when I still had free time, I started to read up on the medieval guilds. All kinds of profession and trades had guilds, organizations of all the members. If you wanted to learn a trade, you could become an apprentice in the guild and afterward you were a guild member forever. Sounds like a union to me."

The laughter was more hesitant.

"One of the differences was that some guilds were not for employees but for the owners. They owed allegiance to each other. They helped each other, cared for each other, loved each other. They were friends and a guild was one of the best kinds of friendship. They were builders and painters and tile makers and so on, but there were no bar men. You know why? No bars. Now we have bars and this is our guild. This is the solid base of our strong friendship. I promise to lead you well, to represent your interests as best I can, and to finish the speech right now because you are all hungry and so am I."

He left the podium to loud applause and raucous cheers, and sat at one of the nearby tables. The applause was short, because the waiters immediately began to serve.

I had listened to his speech because it was short and even interesting. And as I stood back against the wall to keep an eye on the service, I muttered, "Friendship, huh."

The meal went smoothly and I heard compliments as I passed some of the tables. I wasn't exactly holding my breath, but when dessert was served, I was relieved. It was over. Not just the meal. Every meal like this one is an adventure, and this one was more than most, but the convention was over, too. Tomorrow morning they would all leave the hotel for points south and west, except for the few who actually came from Boston and had shared the meals without staying at the hotel. We would all be enormously relieved.

When the hall was finally empty of guests and the final cleanup was in process, I allowed myself the luxury of heading to my office, where I could take my high heeled shoes off and massage my aching feet.

As I passed the door to the reception office, with its glass window, I saw a light inside. The room will always be 'the scene of the crime' for me, but I hadn't realized that the police had left lights on when they finally released the room. I pushed the swinging door open and saw a figure in black bending over what used to be Marshall's desk.

CHAPTER NINETEEN

Rebecca - Wednesday Night

"Excuse me, can I help you?"

The woman started in surprise and turned to face me. She wore a tailored pair of black silk pleated slacks and a figure hugging, low-cut, black sweater. A loose large black beret-like hat hid all of her hair and she wore incongruently comfortable looking lime green running shoes that I realized that I had seen before on a jogger when I was walking down the Mall. Her makeup was perfect with bright red lipstick, high cheekbones, and arched light brown eyebrows. The effect of elegance was spoiled by the gun that she held in her left hand and pointed at me.

With her right hand she pulled off the hat and a mass of blond curls spilled out and covered her shoulders. The first time I had seen her it was only from the back, and that time she had been dressed more or less like a slut. The second time, she had looked entirely different, younger, more athletic and dressed like a jogger, and I had not recognized her. This time I immediately realized who it was. I pretended not to notice the gun in the hope that she would also pretend not to be holding it.

"You're Marshall's wife, widow I mean, aren't you? The last time you were here, you were looking for some documents. My secretary was unable to help you then, but things have changed. Perhaps I can help you now." I said with a smile. I cannot believe how calm I was. I was so close to running screaming out of the office.

"I need some documents that Marshall had, but they are mine, and I need them. I'm looking for them in his desk."

Implied, of course, was that I couldn't do anything about it because she held the gun. There were still some guests in the lobby and the last thing I wanted was this madwoman shooting a gun in the area. Of course, the other very good reason that I wanted to prevent any shooting was because the gun was aimed at me.

"He wouldn't leave private papers here."

"You are just trying to get rid of me, but it won't work. He told me that the papers were here." She looked at me triumphantly.

"He wouldn't leave anything personal or private in this desk because so many people use it. Whenever he's not here, the shift manager, whoever he is, also uses the desk. A locked drawer wouldn't do it."

"So where?"

"The hotel has been using individual safes in each room for many years, but when the hotel opened, there was a bank of safes in reception. You needed two keys to open one. A guest got a key that matched his safe and the receptionist had the other one that was a master key for all the boxes. We still have them and some of us use them, especially receptionists. Sometimes guests prefer them, too. Doubtlessly, that is where Marshall kept his personal documents."

"Where is it?"

"Well, that's the problem. The safes are down below on the floor where the maintenance is."

"Take me there."

"No way."

"You seem to misunderstand me. I have a gun. It has a silencer. I will use it. Since I assume you do not want me to shoot you, you will take me to the bank of safes."

"I don't have the keys."

"Get the one from reception. I have the other one. I just didn't know what it opened." She jabbed me with the gun and for a moment I froze. It wasn't very nice being poked by a revolver, but what chilled me was the proof that she had killed Marshall. I had been pretty sure that the killer was someone that we didn't know but I knew that Marshall had kept the key on a chain around his neck. We all knew. We laughed at him for it, and stupidly, I had never thought to ask the police if it was still there.

I saw her eyes narrow. I feared that she had realized that I knew, and it actually crossed my mind that it could be a good thing to get this crazy murderous woman away from the few people still wandering around on this floor. They were my guests and my staff and I was responsible for them.

"Shall we go to the lobby first and I'll get the key?"

"Don't be silly. Call him. Tell him to bring the key."

I would never ever do that, and Russell knew it. I wasn't sure how he would react and what he would do, but I called him because she didn't give me a choice.

"Rebecca, is everything okay?"

"No. Please bring the master key for the old guest safes right away."

"Yes, ma'am."

While we waited, she chatted with me as if it were a weird sort of social occasion.

"You actually seem to be pretty nice. I wish I had gotten to know you better. Marshall never liked you, but I don't think he had anything specific against you. It was just that his cousin worked in the kitchen and he said that you wrecked a sweet deal that he had going. Marshall was cynical about everyone except for his family and Donald was family."

Donald, huh? That was one puzzle solved, too late to do me much good. She continued the one-sided conversation until Russell knocked lightly on the door and walked in. He took the key out of his pocket, handed it to me and looked at me strangely, but I didn't dare do anything that might set Marshall's widow off on a violent tangent. There was no way to tell him to call the police or even to call Betsy, and I wasn't sure if he got the hint. I fervently hoped that he would realize that if I asked him to leave reception without someone to cover, something was very wrong.

"Shall we go, Mrs. Hammersmith?" I stood and pointed the way out of the office. She followed close behind, too close, with the gun jabbed in my back.

"Don't call me that."

"Well, I have to call you something. Anyway, you really don't need the gun to make me do what I would do with pleasure, anyway."

"Let's just say that it makes me feel safer."

We walked through the empty corridor, our heels clacking on the marble as we approached the elevators. Somewhere in the hotel was a security officer. I only hoped that he would realize that I was in trouble and would not just rush up to greet me, but I couldn't count on it. The elevator door opened and she shoved me towards it, but I stopped and turned towards her. There were still a few guests in the lobby and I was pretty sure that she would not want to arouse their interest.

"If we don't use a staff elevator, we have to use the one on the right. It's the only one that goes down to the basement."

I pushed the button again and the second elevator arrived. We sped downward, to what might be the end of me.

I turned to her again, hoping that I could convince her that I was really quite stupid and did not understand that she was the killer. "I'm really glad to be able to help you. If your husband had something belonging to you, I'll happily help get it. Marshall may have worked here, but I knew that he was not a very nice man. You must have had it really rough."

The elevator reached the bottom and the doors opened. She jabbed me again with the gun.

"Wow, he must really have treated you badly."

"You have no idea."

"Please tell me. Sometimes it helps to get it off your chest."

She ignored my suggestion, and we walked through the dimly lit, empty corridor, passing Betsy's darkened office, then Patsy's, then Maintenance, past the locked double doors where the monstrous electrical transformer lived, past the boiler room, to the end of the space where we had stashed the old safes. They filled a wall with ranks of brown metal doors, each with two keyholes. On the lower left were ten bigger safety boxes, used for large packages. I knew that one of them belonged to Marshall, and I knew that the key that she had taken had no number on it, another obsession that he had explained to us. It had seemed excessively cautious then, but I blessed it now.

She took the key out of her wallet and looked for the number on it.

"Which one is it?"

"Doesn't it have the number stamped on it? They all do."

"This one doesn't." She studied the key. "It looks like there was a number, but it's been filed off. Do you know which it is?"

"No, I don't know. We'll have to check them all. I would start with the top rows. He would want something easy."

"Yeah, that's my Hammer. Here. Take the key and start trying each one. Don't try any funny business. I'm watching."

I began to try the locks, as slowly as I dared, hoping that Russell would call for help.

"Marshall never told me he was married. How did you meet?" I asked in a conversational tone of voice.

Surprisingly, she answered in the same tone. "We're not married any more. We got divorced over ten years ago. We met when we both worked in a hotel in Hyannis on the Cape. He was extremely charming and he bowled me over, but it didn't take long to find out that he was a lying, cheating, sleazy con man. I think that he let me know about his deals and his cons because he thought that I would go along with it, that I would even help him." Her lips curled in remembered revulsion.

"I never got involved in any of his funny business, but I knew too much about him. So when we split, he let me keep the apartment in Hyannis. He had inherited a few apartments from his grandparents, and that was one of them. He even wrote out a signed bill of sale, but he said that he would keep it to make sure I behaved. Ask me what he meant. Go ahead and ask."

"What did he want?" I asked quietly, fearing the answer.

"When he called, I came, usually here, when he had a night shift and the hotel was quiet. He would open his zipper and I would let him come in my mouth. Then I would bend over the desk and he would come at me again. Then he would laugh uproariously, and open the office door for me to walk out. I would leave the hotel, get into my car, and travel south to get home again."

I heard the catch in her throat, and turned around. Tears were streaming down her face.

I kept silent and she continued. "It wasn't so bad most of the time. I could have kept it up, but I met a man. He's a school teacher. He doesn't have much money and he rents a tiny little place, so I need the apartment. I came here, to beg Marshall. He laughed at me, you know. Asked me for a parting party, he said. I did what he wanted, and he laughed again.

Said that he had changed his mind. Said that he was keeping the papers that would have given me my own home because I was too good to give up. Said that he would consider it in a few years if I continued to be a good girl, whenever he wanted. So I shot him. I didn't shoot him to get the documents. That, too, but I really shot him for all those years. All those horrible years."

I found that I, too, had tears in my eyes. She looked at me, sighed, and shook her head.

"You're a nice lady, and I'm sorry, but I have a chance now for a good life, if no one finds out."

"You don't want to kill me."

"You're right, I don't, but I will. Now just keep on looking for the right lock."

She jabbed me again with the gun.

"What is your first name?"

"Why do you care?"

"We are sort of tied together. My name is Rebecca." I wanted to keep her talking.

"Hell, why not. My name is Roberta. Officially, I'm still Hammersmith, but I use my maiden name, Rickert."

"Roberta, it won't work. Your plan to get away with it just won't work. Even if you kill me, the police know. They told me, and I, foolishly, did not believe them."

"And I don't believe you."

She said it with a finality that froze me solid for a minute.

I hoped that if we kept on talking and stalling, help would arrive. The security officer checked this area at least once a night, but I didn't know if he had been here yet.

"How did you do it? Nobody saw you."

"Oh, Marshall planned it well, like always. I always came when there was no doorman and the door was locked. Marshall buzzed me in. Simple as pie."

"But how did you get out? Marshall fell against the door and jammed it."

She looked up and down at my somewhat chubby figure with pity. "I went out through the reception door, locked it behind me with my house key and vaulted over the reception counter. That lock is a joke."

"So you wanted it to look like suicide?"

Her answer was full of disdain. "Even I don't think that the police are that stupid. I kept the gun, so how could it have been suicide? Locking the door was just to make things difficult."

"You do like to do it the hard way."

Her mouth was pursed and her face tight. "Why not? Nobody ever went out of their way to help me, and I needed help. You hotel people are always making a show. Well, there are real people behind that show. Camaraderie? Friendship?

None of that was for me. Now you have to live with it." She laughed bitterly. "Or die with it."

"Why didn't you look for the papers when you were there? Marshall was in no condition to stop you." I hoped that I could ask enough questions to keep her talking.

"I used a home-made silencer, and I was sure that no one heard, but someone's always snooping around. Even guests would sometimes knock on the door and peek in when Marshall locked it for partying, so he would put something over the window, but this time he didn't. I was afraid that I didn't have enough time. I opened the drawer and looked, but I saw only pencils, pens, erasers, and white stickers. There were a bunch of colored forms, but nothing that looked like a document. I thought maybe he glued it to the underside of the drawer, but I was running out of time."

She seemed to want to tell the whole story, and while she was talking, I looked around, hoping that I would see something I could use for a weapon. There was a pile of wooden boards that were intended for the small carpentry shop that we had, but the boards were too long to swing and even if they were not, there was no way to get at them fast enough. She would shoot me first. All I had were two small keys, one in each hand. The only thing I could do with them was to stab her, and the only place I could stab her with any effect was in her eyes. If I didn't hesitate, I could blind her, but if I did hesitate, and I probably would, she would shoot me. Every minute that passed brought me closer to being killed. At some point she would realize that if she shot me, she could look for the right lock herself, and she wouldn't have to listen to my babbling.

She wasn't close enough. If I tried now, she could shoot before I even touched her.

"Hey, I think this is the one."

I was sheltering the view of the safe deposit box with my body. She leaned forward to see and at that instant I did it.

I did hesitate, just enough to miss her eyes, but I hit her cheeks, just below her eyes. She threw up her hands to defend herself, and I threw everything, every bit of strength I had, into hitting the arm that held the gun, and it flew away, landed on the floor and skidded under the pile of boards.

We both dove towards the gun, and we both landed stretched out on the floor. She kicked me, and I kicked back. Within seconds we were rolling on the floor, kicking, scratching, and pulling each other's hair. With my hair wrapped around her right fist, she pulled my head back and grabbed at my throat with her left hand. She released my hair and with both hands she began to squeeze. I tried to pry her hands loose, but she was fit and strong and I was neither. Her face, contorted with fury, loomed above me. Her bright red lipstick and black eye make-up had smudged in the battle between us. There were beads of blood under one eye and a slash that was dripping dark red blood under the other. Her eyes were squinting and her teeth were bared. A drop of sweat rolled off her nose onto my face, followed by a drop of blood, as I flailed around unsuccessfully. Unable to pull her hands away, I felt intense pain and within seconds I couldn't breathe. Bubbles swam across my field of view and I felt weak. I pried at her ring finger on her right hand and was able to get a hold on it. I pulled it back, first a little and then as far as I could, until I heard the bone snap. She howled in anguish, releasing me to cradle her hand. She roared at me, and slapped my face with her good hand. Then, seeing that she was closer to the pile of boards than I was, she stretched out her left hand in an attempt to grab the gun. I bit her. She screamed, twisted back to face me, and socked me in the jaw.

My head flew back and hit the wall. Hard. I didn't see stars. I saw multicolored lights sprinkled all over my field of view. I dimly saw Roberta Rickert Hammersmith crawl over to the gun, pick it up, and point it at me. I dimly heard a voice that sounded like Betsy's shouting "No!" There was a deafening explosion and a slice of hot pain across my forearm. I vaguely saw someone put a gun against my killer's head, and then I was gone.

I woke up to find myself lying on a narrow bed in a tiny room. Hazily, I saw that it was not actually a room, as the walls were only curtains. It was cold, and I realized that a thin inadequate blanket covered me. My head hurt, my arm itched, and my throat was on fire. Looking around in a fog, I saw that everything around me was white, except for the baby blue hospital gown that I was wearing. Then I became aware of the red Harvard sweatshirts that Betsy and Pete were wearing. As clarity began to filter in, I dimly realized that if we were in a curtained enclosure, and not a hospital room, we must be in the emergency room. There was a strong smell of antiseptics. I shook my head, and gasped in pain.

"Oy, that hurt," I croaked.

"I bet it did," Betsy whispered. "Don't do that again. You have a concussion. Don't move too much."

"Concussion? I don't think so. She shot me."

"Yes it is, and no she didn't. The bullet barely scratched you. See?"

She gently lifted my arm to show me a small white pad the size of a Band-Aid, attached below my elbow with strips of plaster. You hit your head really hard and you do have a concussion. Your eye pupils are different sizes, but they've done all kinds of tests while you were out, and nothing is broken. The only symptom you lack is nausea."

I heard her say it, sniffed the sharp, antiseptic, bleach smell around me, felt the nausea and just made it to lean over the side of the bed and throw up on the floor. I leaned back and moaned.

"I am so tired, and my throat hurts like the worst laryngitis ever. I just want to go back to sleep."

Peter answered quickly. "No, no. The doctor said you should keep awake once you regain consciousness. He also said that you probably should try not to talk. She tried to choke you and it's pretty swollen in there."

"Okay, so you tell me a story. How did you find me? I thought I was dead for sure."

Peter went out to find a few chairs, and Betsy leaned on the bed.

"You can sit. There's room."

She sat on the very edge of the bed, and began to speak quietly. "Peter got a call to warn him that Mrs. Hammersmith might be on the way to the hotel. We went to look for you, first, because we saw that your car was still there, but you weren't anywhere we could see. Your office was dark, the banquet was closed up, and we were really puzzled. Peter thought that maybe you had left for home by cab, leaving the Volvo here, so we asked Russell. That is one dumb boy. You will have to do something about him. He told me, with a sweet puzzled expression on his handsome face, that you asked him to bring the master key for the old safes to your office. I was horrified. I asked him if he realized that something was wrong. He said that he asked you on the phone if something was wrong, and you said yes, but when he brought you the key, you were with a guest, and you smiled and thanked him. He was a bit puzzled, so he said. We ran for the staff elevator because it's the most convenient and mostly because it doesn't announce its arrival with a bell. As soon as we hit the bottom floor we heard voices and tiptoed to the end of the corridor just in time to see you get one on the jaw and crash into the wall. The gun fired, but I'm not even sure that she aimed. She didn't hit you, she hit a safe deposit box and the bullet ricochet is what got you. You have a shallow scratch but the safe will never be the same again.

At that moment, Peter returned, dragging two chairs. Betsy got up from the bed, and they both sat next to me. I turned on my side to face them, and the slight movement started a jackhammer banging away inside my brain.

"Sorry it took so long. I saw the doc. He said we could take you home after a few hours, as long as you kept pretty much in bed for the next few days. I figure the hotel would be a better bet. You wouldn't have to do anything for yourself."

"I'll call my mother. If Rebecca stays there, she'll take care of her and no one will bother her. At the hotel, she'll be working from her bed. I don't mean that the way it sounds."

I heard this conversation in a vague confused way. I was so tired. Aside from the time I had been unconscious, I had been on my feet for a very long day.

I whispered, "I don't think I can make it to the morning briefing. Can you do it, Betsy?"

Both them laughed, and Betsy answered patiently, "Bec' dear, you aren't going to any briefing, no time soon. I called Jeri and told her you wanted her to do it."

"Mmph. Wonderful idea, but it's the middle of the night. You didn't have to wake her up."

"Wake up, sleepyhead. You've been unconscious for hours and it's already almost seven. I've called them all so you don't have to worry about doing it. I only gave them a condensed version, but they were pretty much in shock. Jeri just began to cry and the Chef was amazed that such a thing could happen to you."

"Why? Did he think that it should happen to someone else?"

"No, but they all half believe that you're superhuman."

I sighed and mumbled, "A week ago, I half believed it myself. You know, I really feel sorry for Roberta Hammersmith. Marshall did really awful things to her and she was terribly alone. Probably none of this would have happened if she had the support and advice of good friends when she had troubles with Marshall, friends like you guys."

Then I closed my eyes and fell asleep.

Thank you, Reader

I hope that you have enjoyed reading A Conventional Murder and that you will want to read more stories about Rebecca Bauer. As we do in the hotel business, I ask you to tell me if something bothered you and to tell everyone else if it was good. If you can, I would really appreciate a review since books are rated by the number of reviews they receive.

I can be reached at Juliarohatyn@gmail.com and I would love to hear from you. My website can be found at www.juliarohatyn.com

Acknowledgments

I would like to thank Carole Soskis. She was my roommate in college and has been my friend ever since. She read the book, for enjoyment as she said. Then she read it again and did an amazing editing job on it.

A wonderful group of women in Neve Ilan, who have been meeting monthly for almost twenty years, have helped me with some of the editing.

Ellis Shuman, the author of 'Valley of Thracians' and other books, was kind enough to read and critique the book and make several very helpful comments.

Author's Note

I am writing as Julia Rohatyn, not to hide my real name, but to honor my parents. My mother became Judith when she married my father, but remained Julia, the name she had selected when she immigrated to the States, to her sisters, nieces, and nephews for the rest of her life. She was the story teller of the family.

My father told us little about growing up in the town of Rohatyn in the Polish Ukraine until late in life when he joined a group of Rohatyners who rebuilt the Jewish cemetery and contributed to the local population.

My love of books comes from them.

I have been working in hotels for the past forty years, as a general manager for most that time. Hotels are the world in microcosm and so when I began to write mysteries I found a multitude of story ideas in real events. Even so, the hotels in my books are imaginary as are the characters.

I have written several Rebecca Bauer Murder mystery books and I hope to be able to publish them soon on Amazon:

Paper Cuts – Murder at the Allenby

Cold Kills

Murder on Egg Island

Death at a Dude Ranch

Free New Chapter!

Contact me through my website www.juliarohatyn.com or at my email juliarohatyn@gmail.com to register for the VIP list and I will send you a free copy of the first chapter of an oncoming book, and other free chapters as they become available. This list can be the way that I can remain in contact with you, to know what you think and what you would like. I only ask that you review books as they are published as this is the lifeblood of self published authors. I hope that you will enjoy reading 'A Conventional Murder' as much as I enjoyed writing it.

Death at a Dude Ranch

Rebecca Bauer knows a lot about hotels and that is the reason that her boss sends her to check out a dude ranch resort that he wants to buy, but nothing can prepare her for murder. This will be the first time that the proper Bostonian has to solve a crime on horseback.